And a Little Bit More...

Doris Plummer

Acknowledgements

I would like to thank my son Matthew Plummer for the amazing cover he designed for this book.

www.plummerfernandez.com

And Sebastian Kruk for taking a lovely picture of me.

www.sebkphotography.com   email: sebkphoto@gmail.com

I would like to thank, Luis Fernando Mostajo and his lovely wife Anna Poles for their contribution to this book. To my dear friends Ingrid Campo Martinez, Anabella Nader, Martha Bibby, Ana Radcliffe and Ruth Albañez who supported me through this journey and to my dear colleague and friend Lucia Alvarez de Toledo who help me with the corrections and editing of the book.

I find myself looking in a mirror again, into those big black eyes…

Gaby, what is wrong with you, you have achieved everything that you set out to accomplish, your yoga and meditation retreat centre has grown far more than you ever dreamt it would, you have touched lots of many lives, and yet you're still longing for more, I don't understand why this longing never ends, and why can I just be contented with life as it is? I closed my eyes and could feel the tears rolling down my cheeks. I started to meditate trying to calm my longing and to find some inner peace, but I couldn't truly settle down. I thought it was best to just get up and go to the centre, keeping myself busy always helped me forget about my own feelings. I had moved the centre to a house not far from my flat as it had outgrown my living room a long time ago, I still loved my flat, it was the place where I could always come to and withdraw from the world and the sanctuary under the oak tree in my garden always brought me back memories of my time in India, maybe I could go back there for a while, perhaps that's what I was longing for, going back to India.

I arrived at the centre, and it was hectic, Saturdays were always the busiest day, George was already there, we had become the best of friends and partners as we now owned and managed the centre together, but our romance never did flourish, he was looking for a wife to help him raise his daughters and that was not for me. He met a wonderful woman, Lucia; she was from Chile, and they were now married and had a beautiful daughter called Luna. He was a great friend, and we had grown to love each other in a different way, we had a deep spiritual connection, and we shared the same vision to help others grow spiritually, I believe that it was due to this partnership that the centre had become so successful, but success didn't come easy, and we had worked very hard to make it happen. I changed one job because I thought I was working too much only to be working even harder now, but at least it was now working to fulfil my own vision and that was very really rewarding. We had named the centre "Buen Camino" as it reminds us of the Camino de Santiago where we met and where it all started. The centre was set in a very grand old Victorian house, and we had decorated it throughout with ornaments and rugs that my friend Dev Patel had sent from India. We had met when I went there and he and his wife Anika came to visit the centre every time they came to London, they even gave lectures and taught yoga and were much loved by everyone. Dev and George had become close friends, and George had even travelled to India and stayed at his house on a couple of occasions. The centre looked like a mini version of an Indian Ashram and had a wonderfully peaceful atmosphere.

So why on earth was I feeling as if I was missing something? God, I was a difficult woman to please.

"Morning Gaby, how are you today?" asked George as I walked into the centre.

"I'm feeling a bit under the weather, but don't ask me why?"

"Why don't you take the day off, invite your friend Linda to have a girl's day out, go shopping, go to the hairdressers, buy some Prosecco; take some time for yourself; I can manage on my own."

"That sounds great; I think I need some "me" time. Are you sure you don't need me here; it looks very busy?"

"Go away, and don't come back until you have a happier face."

I called Linda, and we arranged to meet for lunch at a restaurant in trendy Notting Hill, we could walk first around the market, I loved the atmosphere of it, filled with tourists and all the stalls selling antiques, food, and clothes. The place transported me to other the markets around the world, they all have a happy atmosphere around them.

I met Linda by the tube station, she was my best friend, we had met at my previous job; she was looking gorgeous in a blue summer's dress that suited her new slimmer figure, with her long black hair, and her usual lovely smile.

"Hello, darling how lovely to see you, I nearly fainted when you called asking me to meet you on a Saturday, fancy you taking a day off."

"I need some time for myself and couldn't think of a better way to spend it than here with you." We gave each other a big hug and walked out of the station together, it was an unusually warm summer's day in

London, the sun was shining and the crowds were out in full. We bought pretty enamel brooches from one of the stalls, I chose a blue butterfly and Linda went for a red ladybug, we then went to the Italian restaurant I had booked a table and ordered a bottle of Prosecco.

"Cheers, my friend this has been a wonderful idea, we should do it more often," I said to Linda with a big smile, going out had changed me completely I was now very happy and thought that maybe I could do with a holiday, going back to India was high in the agenda, but maybe I could try somewhere new.

"How is your work and how is Tom, is he still making you work hard?"

"Tom spends now most of his time playing golf whilst I'm basically running the place by myself and working harder than ever, but to be honest now that my sons have left home to go to Uni, I rather stay late at the office than going back home to an empty house. But I could do with a short break, especially now that is very quiet at work and the weather is so nice."

"Taking the day off has made me realize that maybe I need a break too; why don't we go next weekend to Glastonbury, it's a bank holiday, and we could leave on Friday to avoid the traffic, what do you think?" I said enthusiastically to Linda.

"That sounds great. I love Glastonbury with all the esoteric shops and Tor, and the old ruined cathedral, and all the stories about King Arthur and the Knights of the Round Table. I am sure Tom can stay one day in the office without playing his beloved golf."

"I'm sure George won't mind either, he has taken lots of time off, when the baby was born and whilst traveling, that's the benefit of having a partner to share the running of the centre."

We looked on the internet on our mobile phones and booked a room in the Shekin Ashram on the foothills of Tor.

We spent the rest of the afternoon planning our trip and giggling a lot, we were quite tipsy when we left after having drunk two bottles of our favourite bubbly.

Early on Friday morning, Linda arrived to pick me up in a brand new 4x4 Range Rover.

"Wow, Linda, this is a rather nice car?"

"This is one of the perks of nearly running the place and Tom does treat me a lot as he gets more frightened of me leaving him than anything else in the world, and that's why he didn't say anything when I told him I was taken the day off."

"I am not complaining, we deserve to travel in style, but I can sense that there is more to you and Tom's story?" I could see Linda going bright red, and she nearly crashed the brand-new car.

"I was going to tell you, but I didn't know how, I know we always said that never with a married man, but it just happened, and now it's gone far too long, and I can't stop it." Linda said, nearly choking.

"You know he will never leave his wife, don't you?"

"I know that," she said, really sobbing now.

"He is not just using you, is he?"

"No! We are happy and we both know that he will never leave his family, but the time that we spend together is wonderful, and he does treat me really well."

"Well, I won't ever mention it again, but no wonder you are so slim and glowing, maybe I should have tried going out with him when I used to work there." I said, laughing, and Linda just gave me "the look."

I put the radio on and one of our favourite songs from the M People came on "Search for the Hero" and we started singing out loud "search for the hero inside yourself until you find the key to your life."

From then on, we just kept on singing and laughing and nothing was going to spoil our lovely weekend. It was wonderful getting out of London; I love the English countryside, so green and postcard-perfect. Once we left the motorway, I opened the window and let the wind blow into my face, and then on the right-hand side, I could see Stonehenge at a distance.

"Why don't we stop here for a rest and have a look around the stones, it's been a while since I last came here," I said to Linda.

"That's a great idea; I could do with a coffee, and what better way to stretch my legs than that walking around Stonehenge."

We started searching for the way in but couldn't find it.

"This has changed a lot since the last time I was here, I came when the boys were young and the entrance was quite close to the stones."

"We better follow the signs as nothing looks familiar to me either."

We went a long way round until we found the entrance, as we went in there was now a large cafeteria, museum, and store and there was now a small train taking you close to the stones; I thought I was in Disneyland and not in Stonehenge, but still, it was all very well organized. We bought two cappuccinos, and we took the next train to the stones. As we arrived there, we were ushered into a path that goes around them and you are not allowed to touch them anymore.

"I remember when I first came here with my family, and we could touch them and jump all over the stones."

"I remember that too, but back then Stonehenge wasn't so famous and there were not so many tourists, I suppose that if they had continued to allow people near the stones the sight would have been destroyed."

I just started walking admiring this fabulous prehistoric monument - one of the most famous landmarks in the UK that stands like none other in the Salisbury Plains in Wiltshire, a place that never ceases to amaze me and all the visitors that come here every year. There are so many theories surrounding it, some say it was built by the Druids for ceremonial purposes and some even say that it was built by extra-terrestrials. I suppose that we will never truly know why it was ever built, like so many other mysteries around the world, but for now, all I could do was admire it.

We got back to the car and headed to Glastonbury, and then Linda just looked at me…

"Now Gaby, it's your turn to tell me about your love life, because I can't believe that you have given up, as I can't picture you like a well-behaved nun."

It was my turn to blush.

"There isn't much that you don't know, when things didn't work out romantically with George and as Peter kept calling; I finally gave in, and we are now seeing each other, he might not be the love of my life, but we enjoy each other's company, and he keeps me young, but I can't see myself ever settling down, not with him or anyone else."

"And what happened with the gorgeous German guy that you said was the spitting image of Brad Pitt, he sounded very promising?"

"Wagner, we have seen each other a few times, once here in London and I went to Düsseldorf a couple of times, but there is no chance of me going to live there and nor will he ever come to live to London, so as much as we like each other that is never going to happen."

"I thought you might have left him because of his name, who is going to date someone called Wagner?"

"Linda! Your mum should have called you Agnes," I said laughing at her.

Well, will see what the future brings us, we might end up the two of us together as old ladies, drinking Prosecco, but for now keep looking at the road signs as I have lost the GPS signal, and we are not far from our destination."

I was looking at the road when suddenly after a bend there it was, Tor with the St Michael's Tower standing majestically at the top. I pointed it to Linda, and she had to stop for a minute just to admire it as Glastonbury Tor is known as being one of the most spiritual sites in the country, and it does take your breath away. We drove slowly through the beautiful town until we reached the Ashram.

I was pleasantly surprised to see a set of Tibetan prayer wheels at the entrance of the Ashram; I immediately turned them and imagined that I was back in the Himalayas.

"Namaste, welcome to Shekim Ashram," said a lovely lady dressed in an Indian sari."

"Namaste, what a lovely place, we have a reservation for two, we are Gaby and Linda" I replied to her.

"My name is Linzy, I was expecting you, I will show you to your room, you were very lucky to find a space as being bank holiday we have been fully booked for a while and when a couple cancelled, I noticed that your booking came immediately after."

"I suppose we were meant to be here; I have learned that there are no coincidences in life," I said, smiling at her.

"Is there anything special going on?" asked Linda.

"There is a talk tonight in the main hall given by a gentleman from Bolivia. Here, take a leaflet" Linzy said, handing us a copy. "But let me show you to your room first".

We followed her, and she took us to a quite basic room with two small beds in the middle of the room.

There were lots of Indian figurines and a great big picture of Buddha on the wall and when she opened the window, we had a magnificent view of Tor.

"You are very lucky; this room has the best views," she said, smiling. "Breakfast is from 8 until 10 am, is vegan and self-service. There is also a sauna, but I'm afraid it is already fully booked for the weekend." She handed us the keys and left.

"Lets' go straight out to find a place to eat, I'm starving," Linda said to me and as I was also famished, I just grabbed my handbag and the leaflet that Linzy had given us as I wanted to read about the guy that was giving the talk that evening.

We walked down the high street looking at all the shops, full of crystals and any esoteric ornament you can think of, and also lots of places offering tarot readings, psychics, palmistry, numerology, and all sort of sorceresses.

"We must book a reading for later on."

We inquired in a few places, but it was all fully booked, so in the end, we went into a nice vegetarian restaurant, and we sat and had our late lunch. There was a very large group at the far end of the place and there I seemed to recognize someone, his face looked familiar, and then I looked at the leaflet Linzy had given us, and it was a picture of the man sitting at that table.

"He is rather good-looking; I wouldn't have expected that, when Linzy mentioned that he was from Bolivia I thought he would be a short native Indian Shaman. It says here that he has contact with extra-terrestrials, I've never been too much into ETs but now that I have seen him, we better make sure that we get back in time to the Ashram for his talk this evening."

"Gaby, never judge a book by its cover, you don't know anything about ETs and now just because he is good-looking you seem to have gained a lot of interest in the subject; you will never ever change." We both burst out laughing.

When we finished our lunch, we went for a walk around the town, we thought it was best to visit the Abbey and the Chalice Wells and all other places of interest the following days as it had been a rather long drive for Linda. We walked into one of the alleys that have lots of nice shops and at the top there was a one called the Goddesses Temple. We went in and we were asked to take our shoes of leave all our belongings by the entrance. it was quite a large room and, in the middle, there was a round temple surrounded by human size women made of straw and right in the middle there was a beautiful painting of the lady of Avalon dressed in blue, with golden hair and rays of light coming out from her heart. A few minutes later, a beautiful woman that resembled the painting walked into the temple, she had long pink shining hair, and was wearing a long white dress.

"Hello, ladies I am one of the goddesses that guard this temple, we train here in Glastonbury for many years and we do healing rituals here at the temple, and if you would like to join us we are going to perform a small ceremony right now." Both Linda and I nodded, we were soon joined by another three ladies, one of them laid down in the middle and the rest of us surrounded her, the lady in the white robe laid some crystals on top of the lady that was in the middle; she then held a bowl with burning incense and on the other hand she was holding three large feathers, she started singing the most beautiful song about returning home to Avalon and I felt that I was coming home too. She placed the bowl in front of each of us and with the feathers she bathed us with the incense smoke. She then held a large Tibetan bowl with her left hand and a mallet with her right hand and she softly moved the mallet around the bowl that produced a very high pleasant rich tone, she kept on singing and at the end she asked as to chant a few OM's with her. She then removed the crystals from the lady in the middle and we all hugged.

"Thank you, ladies, for staying, meditation and healing are always best carried out by large numbers as the energy will increase and I could feel there was a lot of energy here today."

"Thank you for allowing as to stay here, it was an amazing experience," said Linda and I was startled as I could see she was genuinely moved by it all. We stayed there for a short while taking it all in and we then left.

We strolled around the backstreets when we came across a rather spooky shop - the window had spiders and a rather large skeleton but on the corner of the display was a small sign "Tarot card and psychic readings."

"Let's try here," I asked Linda.

"No chance, this looks too scary."

But I took no notice of her and just went straight in. There were a couple of young guys with long hair, a few tattoos, and one had a top hat.

"What can we do for you?" asked the one with the top hat.

"I was wondering if we can book an appointment each for a Tarot card reading."

"Yes, as a matter of fact, we were let down by a couple, and we do happen to have the next hour free; it's £20 for half an hour."

I followed the guy to a back room and Linda stayed looking around the shop. I didn't even look at her because I knew that she was about to give me the look.

The room was less spooky than the rest of the shop and in one corner there was a huge statue of the Virgin Mary that immediately calmed me down.

"My name is Jamie, what brings you here today?"

"Nothing in particular."

"So, just a general throw." He took a package of Tarot cards and handed them to me.

"Please shuffle the cards thoroughly and when you are done divide them into three piles." I did as he instructed, "Now, chose one of the three." I gave him the pile I had chosen and he started to deal the cards. The first card that came out was the 8 of Wands.

"You are going on a long journey."

"I am thinking about it but, maybe going back to India, but it won't be for too long, I have a business to run." He dealt another card, and it was the 2 of Pentacles. "This is a very positive card for your business, it's very prosperous, and it will steadily grow, he dealt a few more cards, the last one being the Wheel of Fortune."

"Don't worry about your business it looks as if you have a very good team working with you, but I do see a very long voyage, and it would be a new destination and very far away. He kept dealing more cards. "It will be good for you and I can see the Page of Swords, there might be a young man on the scene."

I blushed and thanked him.

I asked Linda, and she went in whilst I stayed looking around the shop and talking to the other guy. They were much nicer and less scary than they pretended to be.

Linda came back out later, smiling and looking rather pleased.

"Jamie thinks I might get pregnant, but I told him it was more probable for me to be a grandmother than to become a mother again. We shouldn't waste our money honestly". We burst out laughing, and then I caught sight of the time in the church clock and I told Linda that we should go back, or we wouldn't make it in time to the talk.

We arrived at the centre and went straight to the main hall, there were quite a few people in there already, we sat on some cushions quite close to the main stage and a few minutes later the tall guy that we had seen at the restaurant walked in and sat at the front.

The room was now full; I was quite surprised to see so many people interested in ETs.

"Hello, I'm Luis Fernando Mostajo Maertens, I'm from Bolivia.

He said in a very strong Spanish accent and struggling to speak English.

Linzy stepped in and said that although Luis Fernando could speak some English it was hard for him to give the whole talk in it, but unfortunately, they had been let down by the Spanish Interpreter they had booked.

I raised my hand and said:

"Maybe I can help, I can speak Spanish, and although I am not a proper interpreter, I could give it a try."

Luis Fernando gave me a big smile and with a big expression of relief on his face just said.

"Si, por favor."

"Yes, please."

I went and sat next to him and everybody clapped. Luis Fernando started talking about his experiences and contacts with extra-terrestrials and with people from Venus, it was very interesting and everyone paid a lot of attention. When he finished, he said he was going to walk to the Tor and that everyone was welcome to go up with him for an evening meditation.

I went back to my room, to put on a coat, as it would probably get cold up at the top of the mountain. Linda was already in bed and when I asked her if she wanted to go. She just looked at me.

"Not in a million years, I will probably fall asleep as soon as the meditation starts, take some photos of the ETs if they do show up," she said, smiling.

I grabbed my coat and a scarf and left.

I went to the main entrance and there was a small group of people gathered there as soon as Luis Fernando arrived, we started to climb up the Tor. We walked quietly until we reached St Michael's Tower: a magnificent gothic tower that stands at the top, and the view from up there were absolutely amazing there was stills some light and a gentle breeze. Luis Fernando asked everyone to hold hands around the tower and some other people who were up there joined in, there were also some people playing music and chanting, and we started walking clockwise around the tower. We went around three times and then Luis Fernando started a guided meditation and finished by chanting "OM" several times, then suddenly he said:

"Look" pointing at some very bright lights up in the sky, they were moving around and suddenly one stopped and sent a bolt of lightning, and then, they all disappeared, just like that in a wink of an eye.

"They are just letting us know, that they are there and that the work that we are doing here is very important."

I was absolutely blown away and gobsmacked. On the way down, everyone was talking and nobody could hold their excitement.

I tried to wake up Linda when I arrived back at the Ashram, but she just turned around and hid under her quilt and I just stayed there staring at the ceiling trying to digest what I had witnessed that evening.

When I woke up, Linda had already gone downstairs for breakfast; I put something on and dashed to the dining room. I found her sitting at a table, already enjoying breakfast.

"Sorry, I was so hungry, and I just couldn't wake you up."

"That's a huge breakfast; I hope you are not eating for two?" I winked at her.

"Hahaha, don't even mention it, now, tell me all about last night's UFO quest."

I sat down and told her all about it.

"Those were probably planes or helicopters from an army base around here."

"They couldn't have been moving backward and forwards and then just suddenly disappearing into thin air."

Linda wouldn't budge, "I will have to see it to believe it, maybe next time I'll come with you."

"Buenos días chicas," said Luis Fernando as he approached our table.

"Buenos días, Luis Fernando, how are you this morning?"

"Muy bien," he said with a big smile and then asked me if I could be so kind to interpret for him that day as they were going to visit the abbey and the Chalice Wells.

I gave an approving node to Linda and just said:

"We were going there anyway, and would be delighted to help you out."

"Gracias," he said, giving me a relief sight.

"Will be leaving in about half an hour."

I could sense that Linda wasn't quite happy about it.

"Come on Linda, spit it out."

"I thought we were coming here to spend the weekend together, and since you saw this man, you haven't paid any attention to me."

"I didn't exactly plan any of this, you've seen how things have unfolded and by now you should know that..."

"Things happen for a reason" Linda finished my phrase "You are not falling for this guy, are you?"

"No, he is different, there is something very special about him, but it's more like a guru, I have the same feeling I had when I met Dev Patel - as if I am in the presence of someone very special."

"Okay, let's go but don't forget I exist."

"After breakfast, we made our way to the main entrance and met up with a group of around 20 people, and we all started walking towards Glastonbury Abbey. On our way to the Abbey, Luis Fernando was telling us the stories and the myths of the Abbey.

"The Abbey was one of the most prominent and wealthiest Monasteries in the Kingdom but was unfortunately demolished during the dissolution of the Monasteries under King Henry VIII" said Luis Fernando in Spanish and I just translated it for everyone.

"The importance of Glastonbury is directly linked with Joseph of Arimathea, who was a wealthy follower of Jesus Christ and who buried his body in his own tomb after the Crucifixion. It is believed that Jesus gave Joseph the Holy Grail, the cup used by him at the Last Supper and after the Crucifixion Joseph travelled here to Glastonbury and buried the Grail in a secret place just below the Tor; later on, water began emanating from it; the spring is now known as the Chalice Wells. King Arthur and the Knights of the Round Table came here searching for the Grail, and when Arthur died, the knights buried him here at the Abbey."

"Of all places in the world, why here in Glastonbury?"asked someone in the group.

"The legend also says that Joseph travelled here with a teenage Jesus and together began building the Abbey, and so he returned with the Grail and buried it here."

We arrived at the Abbey and when I went to get the tickets, Luis Fernando stopped me'.

"The entrance to all the places we visit is on me, that is the least I can do for all the help you are giving me."

"Gracias" I said to Luis Fernando. I glanced and winked at Linda, we were being given a history lesson and entrances to all places for free.

As we walked into the Abbey I immediately felt very much at peace, the ruins of the Abbey are set within beautiful gardens. We all walked and stood in front of where King Arthur and Guinevere are supposed to be buried, and I could just feel their presence, I closed my eyes and imagined what it must have been like in the times of Avalon, Merlin, and Guinevere and a graceful King Arthur riding in his white horse, it must have been a magical era. I was brought back from my dream state by Luis Fernando, asking me to translate a few words for him.

"The Holy Grail represents the union with the Holy Presence of the Christ, and that is why we can all feel so much his presence here in Glastonbury."

We then all walk down a set of stairs, and we reached St Mary's Chapel which is set in the basement of the ruins. There Luis Fernando asked us to hold hands around the altar and guided us in a short meditation. "We give thanks for our guides that have brought us here and allowed us to enrich our souls with the energy of the Holy Grail, Amen".

"Amen.", said everyone in unison, and we left as there were quite a few tourists staring at us.

We walked out of the Abbey and had lunch in one of the quaint vegetarian restaurants in the high street, and afterward, we strolled to the Chalice Well.

Set a bit back from the main street we found the entrance to the Chalice Well, we walked through a tunnel made of wood and trees and flowers, and as you walk past the main gate; you enter the most beautiful gardens, with a stream right in the middle, and a few wider ponds at the end of it. There are a few paths made of stones for people to walk around it, all surrounded by very lush green vegetation, with a few aromatic flowers dotted around the garden, giving it a very sweet aroma. All of the stream is red in colour given by the high contents of iron in the water and given rise to the myth that this is the blood of Christ, emanating from the buried Chalice deep down in the earth. Where the actual well is, there is a stone circle around it and the well is covered by a round wooden door adorned with wrought iron Vesica Pisces, an ancient sacred symbol of two interlocking circles, its geometry symbolizes a union, of heaven and earth; the ornament also bears a heart at the top and some decorative flowers on the sides of it. We sat down around the well and Luis Fernando started saying:

"Glastonbury is considered to be the heart chakra of Mother Earth and sitting here by the Chalice Well probably means that we are sitting right in the middle of the heart of the Earth, this is one of the most sacred places on this planet, so I will advise you all to close your eyes and meditate reflecting on that."

It was very peaceful sitting there listening to the sound of the water in such a special place. After a while, we opened our eyes, and we walked a little further to where the water actually starts coming out from the head of a stone lion set in a small wall of stone bricks. There were a few people queuing to get water as people come from all over the world since it is supposed to have healing powers.

I said to Linda that we should try and get as much water as we could, we drank a lot directly from the fountain and we filled a couple of plastic bottles each. We all stayed there enjoying the gardens, I took my shoes off and put my feet in the water, and a few children were doing the same playing and laughing in that enchanting place.

After a while Luis Fernando said that we should get ready as we were going right next door to the other well, the one from a white spring that it was in a cave around the corner from the Chalice Well.

"This is the Masculine well representing the Chris and the other one is the Female spring embodying the essence of Mary Magdalene, Glastonbury is also crossed by the Ley lines of St Michael and Mary Magdalene, and as you know the tower at the top of Tor is St Michael's Tower, the guardian of the Mystical Isle of Avalon."

At that point, Linda looked at me and gestured to me that she wasn't going anywhere else.

"Why not?" I asked her.

"To be honest, all this is too much for me, and I am pretty tired of it all. I'll wait for you at the Ashram, I am feeling quite drowsy."

"Okay, as soon as we finish, I'll go to the Ashram too, and we can go out later on just the two of us for dinner and a glass of Prosecco."

Linda gave me a big smile and she left.

The other well was literally next to the Chalice Well, on the next road going up towards the Tor. There in the middle of the stone was a small doorway leading to a series of caves. I was a bit hesitant as the dark cave frightened me.

"The cave you fear to enter holds the treasure you seek," said Luis Fernando as he was right behind me. I looked at him and went straight in, the caves were lit with many candles giving the whole place an enchanted atmosphere, I became overwhelmed and shed a tear or two, I had a feeling that something inside of me was changing, and I had the feeling I was in the right place. We just stayed there for a few minutes, and then we all went out. At that point the group dissolved, some wanted to go back to the shops and some wanted to go up to the Tor. I said goodbye to everyone and started walking back to the Ashram; when I felt Luis Fernando running behind me.

"Thanks for all your help; tomorrow we are driving to Avebury as it's another mystical place in England and to see if we can see a Crop Circle as it's the area where they appear, I would love you and Linda to come and join us."

"I would love to go, but I will have to ask Linda, I am afraid I am in her hands as we drove here in her car, and she is not much into these things, she is a lovely friend, good-hearted but not much into spirituality and I know she is struggling with all this information," I said looking at him with pleading eyes, as I would love to go.

"I think we might be able to squeeze you into one of our cars if you really want to go to Avebury, we are only staying there one night."

"I'll talk to Linda and will let you know later on." We arrived at the Ashram and I went straight to my room.

Linda was fast asleep, I was rather worried about her, she was usually full of energy, but she looked very rundown, I was sure that Tom had been making her work all hours of night and day, and God knows what else if they were seeing each other after work. I always thought of him as an energy vampire and right now it looked as if he had sucked all of my dear friend's energy.

I lay in my bed for a while but there was no sign of Linda waking up and I was getting very hungry so I decided to go downstairs to the restaurant; I ordered some food and as I was starting to eat Linda turned up.

"Why didn't you wake me up, I thought we were going out?"

"You were fast asleep, and I didn't have the heart to wake you up, come and join me, order some food, it's very nice, although it's all vegetarian, and they don't sell Prosecco." I gave her a big smile, hoping she wouldn't get cross with me. Linda reluctantly sat down and ordered some food.

"I needed that sleep, I am not feeling well lately, I do get tired easily and don't have much energy to do anything, I think it must be the menopause, I am at that age, besides I haven't had my period for a couple of months."

"Promise me you will go and see your GP as soon as we get back."

"Promise."

At that moment, Luis Fernando appeared.

"You mind if I join you?"

"Please sit down, Linda just ordered her dinner, you can order yours, and we can all have dinner together."

"Most of the people from my group went up the Tor, I think they are all hoping to catch another glimpse from our friends from the sky, but I am rather tired, I am still jet-lagged. Have you mentioned anything to Linda about Avebury?"

"What about Avebury?" Linda said immediately.

"Luis Fernando and his group are driving tomorrow to the Avebury Stone Circle to see if we can see a Crop Circle." I said to her.

"I will have to go back to London, I don't think I can take another day off from work, but you go, I know it would love to be there as you love all these kinds of things. Have you told Luis Fernando about your yoga centre and all the talks people give there, maybe he can give a talk about UFOs when you get back to London?

"Are you sure you won't mind me going to Avebury?"

"Absolutely, I will drive straight home and I know you will always regret it if you don't go." She gave me a very reassuring look.

Dinner arrived, and I told Luis Fernando all about my travels and about the yoga centre.

"That's it, you must come to Bolivia. I would love to show you all the sacred places like Tiwanaku, Lake Titicaca, and so on."

Linda interrupted:

"You see, you were thinking of where to go next, and there you have it, Bolivia, sounds like a very exciting place."

"It sounds really tempting, let me think about it, but let's go to bed now, it's been a long day, and we have a long drive tomorrow."

I said goodbye to Linda, I felt unease about letting her drive back to London all by herself but, on the other hand, I really wanted to go to Avebury and maybe Bolivia…

It took a few hours to get to Avebury, but it was interesting to listen to all the stories everyone had about UFOs. We arrived at a very traditional black and white Elizabethan Pub that was also a hotel; at that point I remembered I had not booked anything.

"Oh dear, where am I going to stay?"

"Don't worry we still have the room booked for the interpreter that never turned up, it's all paid for, so you are in luck", said one of the English ladies that had organized the event.

"For a minute I thought I would have to sleep in one of the cars."

"Let's drop our things in our rooms and let's meet back here in 20 minutes, we don't have much time here in Avebury," said Luis Fernando.

Twenty minutes later we all met up and walked together just across the road from the pub to the stone circles that consist of three circles, a larger one that contains two smaller inner circles. This is one of the largest stone circles in the world set partially around the village of Avebury and you can actually walk right next to the stones. Some stones are huge and one wonders how on earth they managed to move those stones in the Neolithic era when they were built. It is a lovely setting in a field with lots of people walking around them, some families having picnics and all in all it was a very English countryside atmosphere. We walked around the stones some people meditated and at the end we went to a small shop next to the stones that has a map where all the Crop Circles in the area have recently appeared.

"At the moment there is only a round large crop circle, it's right next to Silbury Hill which is the largest prehistoric monument in Europe that is a man-made hill and you can walk up to the top and from there you can see the circle but it's not a very elaborate one; come back tomorrow, every morning I take a good look around the area with my drone to see if any have come up."

"Great, thanks, see you tomorrow," I said to the shop owner.

We then walked around the village, a very pretty small stone-built quirky place with a beautiful church in the middle and a large country manor on one end, all surrounded by very lush gardens. It was a lovely summer evening, a perfect setting just to stroll around. I was amazed by the beauty of it all.

Early the next morning, as we were about to have breakfast, the owner of the shop across the road came running in.

"There's a new amazing Crop Circle formation that has appeared this morning," he said very excitedly, showing us an image taken by his drone. We all stood up and started running outside.

"It's only about a 15 minutes' drive from here, follow me, I'll go on my motorbike," said the elated man.

We run into our cars and followed him, and after a few minutes' drive to the left of the road in a deep valley we could see the Crop Circle, it was a series of round circles in the shape of a letter S and with a head to one end, and a tail to the other resembling a Dragon. We stopped and parked at the edge of the road and run down towards the crop formation, Luis Fernando took his mobile phone out and started filming. When he looked at what he had just filmed, there appeared to be some very bright lights hovering above the formation.

"They are still here, they haven't quite finished" he shouted. We all stood still and watched the short film.

"What are they?"

"Canoplas". They are called intelligent energies, programmed the same way as a printer on paper; they operate in 5D on the field, modifying the vibrational levels in the area as portals. You could say they are like energy drones."

We kept on running until we reached the Crop Circle, as soon as I arrived, I could feel goose bumps all over my body, I looked at everyone else and could sense that we were all feeling the same thing; there was clearly an energy field.

"All take a deep breath and allow your bodies to absorb this energy," said Luis Fernando. The sun was just starting to come out and the sun rays mixed with the energy from the dragon crop circle formation made me feel a bit dizzy and I had hot flashes all over my body; I laid down on top of the wheat springs, I closed my eyes and after a few minutes I heard a loud noise. There was a man in a tractor and a few others walking next to it and some had rifles pointing at us.

"You are trespassing, this is private land, get out of here.", a man was shouting waving at us, we all started running toward the cars and when we reached them, we wept as we watched as the tractor destroy this wonderful dragon formation. We only had the film Luis Fernando had taken and the photographs from the drones to evoke that magnificent Crop Circle.

We went back to the Pub, gathered our belongings, and headed back to London.

A few days later, Luis Fernando gave a talk in the centre about UFOs and our experiences in the magical mystery places of Avebury and Avalon.

I gave him a big hug, and he made me promise I would visit him in Bolivia.

It all happened very fast after that, George virtually pushed me to book the flights, Lucia, his wife said that I should fly to Chile first and stay with her family and from there I could travel on to Bolivia.

"And as you are already in South America, you must visit Peru and Machu Pichu," said Lucia with a big grin on her face.

I looked at George, and he just said "Don't look at me, just go; I am sure I can manage by myself; I will take a longer holiday when you come back." I booked my flights, first to Chile and then to Bolivia and Peru.

The next few days were very hectic getting ready for my big adventure. I invited Linda out to dinner the evening before my flight. I booked a lovely Italian restaurant close to my house, and as I ordered a bottle of Prosecco, Linda said:

"Just order a glass for yourself, I'm not drinking alcohol."

"Why not?" I said rather surprised as I knew she would never, ever, miss a chance of a glass of our favourite bubbly.

"I'm pregnant!"

"Oh no, how come?" I said utterly surprised and in a state of shock.

"Well, I don't have to explain to you how one gets pregnant, but at my age and with two grown-up sons, I can't bear it, I don't know what I am going to do," she said now crying out loud. I sat next to her putting my arms around her,

"Have you told Tom?"

"Not yet, I know he is going to kill me, I actually went to have an abortion this morning, but I couldn't go through with it."

"Why didn't you tell me I could have gone with you," I said, looking quite annoyed at her.

"You were too busy arranging your trip."

"Oh dear, I am sorry I haven't been there for you when you clearly needed me the most, but I had no idea, and now I am flying tomorrow morning I feel bad leaving you like this."

"Can I borrow your flat whilst you are away? I might need a place to hide."

"No need to ask anything I can do for you, but promise me you will tell Tom."

"Well, I will have to as it's going to start showing soon, I am three months pregnant."

"So, you've made up you are having it" I said inquisitively.

"Yes, I am, I will tell the boys first and then Tom."

"And, the fortune-teller was right about everything, we must go and see him again when I come back," I said to Linda and we both giggled like school children.

"Send me a daily text; let me know how you are feeling, what the boys say and Tom's reaction". A million things were crossing my mind and when my glass of Prosecco arrived, I lifted it up and made a toast to the health of the baby and my wonderful friend.

Chile

Travelling to Chile is not for the faint-hearted: it's such a long flight I think I had breakfast, lunch, and dinner twice, I run out of movies to watch and sleeping in a flight full of children running up and down the aisle is an impossible task; when the pilot finally announced that we were descending I got really excited, but it took another half hour for the plane to leave the Andes, having to fly deep into the South Pacific and then flying back to be able to land. The view from my window was amazing, and it reminded me of the view from the plane back in the Himalayas, I don't know why but chain mountains are so mesmerizing, more so to someone like me that lives in England where we have hardly any mountains and nothing compared to the majestic Himalayas or the Andes. After clearing immigration and collecting my bags I walked out and there standing with a placard with Gaby written on it was a mini version of Lucia. I gave her a big hug.

"Welcome to Santiago," said Margarita, with a big broad smile, she was very slim with long brown hair and was wearing a beautiful summer dress. I was wearing my winter clothes and coat and there it hit me, I was in the farthest country in South America, such a long way from home, they were in the middle of their summer and we in the coldest part of the year.

We walked to her car, a brand new 4x4, and she drove down a very up-to-date motorway, we then drove past near the city centre with lots of very tall skyscrapers. I was gobsmacked. Margarita looked at me and, sensing that I was a bit surprised by it all, just said:

"We call it "Sainthattan" like "Manhattan", too many skyscrapers for my liking, especially as we have so many earthquakes here in Chile, and when one of them catches you right at the top of one of those buildings, it's very scary, they swivel backwards and forwards, and it gives me the creeps, even though they have been built to sustain such movements."

"I hope you don't live in one of those? I don't think I could sleep." I said laughing.

"Don't worry, I live in a bungalow in the outskirts of Santiago, I wouldn't like to live in one of those either."

We finally arrived at her house, I was expecting a small English countryside-type bungalow, but this was a huge modernist white Le Corbusier style house, with huge glass window panels and beautiful lush gardens all around it.

"Welcome to my home," said Margarita and as she came down the 4x4 a couple of golden retrievers came running to greet us.

"These are Frida and Diego, like the Mexican artists, but worth more than any of their paintings to me."

We walked into a very modernist house, very tastefully decorated.

"I'll take you to your room, no doubt you would like to take a shower and maybe have something to eat."

"No more food please I must have eaten everything they had on the plane, as there was not much else to do, but would really appreciate a nice shower and a rest, I am exhausted."

I was taken to a lovely modern bedroom; it had a bathroom, and a huge TV, with a set of sliding doors leading into the garden.

"This looks better than any hotel room, thank you."

"Thank you, I like to keep a nice room for my friends that come and visit."

A maid brought my luggage in and helped me to unpack; I felt a bit like in a modern times Downton Abbey. I woke up later on in the middle of the night, I must have slept for twenty-four hours and felt disorientated, and I opened the sliding doors and stepped into the garden. Diego and Frida came to greet me. I looked into the sky and I had never seen so many stars; the sky was very clear and was amazing, just like in the Himalayas.

"Hello sleeping beauty, I hope you had a good rest," said Margarita with a big smile.

"What time is it? I hope I didn't wake you up."

"It's 11 o'clock, time to go to bed" she winked at me, "come on let's go to the kitchen and I'll give you something to eat now, you must be starving; Lucia said you are mainly vegetarian but that you eat fish, so I have some of Chile's favourite dishes, as we have such an extensive seafront, we do eat a lot of seafood."

"These are Parmesan Machas, a pink clam topped with Parmesan cheese, my favourite."

They were absolutely delicious, and something I had never eaten before, I ate lots and I told her all about her sister and George and Luna and the yoga centre.

"I would love to come and visit you one day, but the dogs and my work keep me tied up here."

"What do you do for a living?"

"Didn't Lucia tell you?" she said a bit surprised, "I am an animal communicator, I talk to animals."

"That sounds amazing, Lucia never said anything to me, and she knows I am open to anything, please tell me all about it," I said with my eyes wide open and paying full attention.

"I've always liked animals, my house was always full of them; we had cats, dogs, hamsters, chickens; you name it, we had them all, my mother must have been like me that she could "talk" to animals as she loved them all. As I grew older, I knew that I could sense what the animals were saying, it's difficult to explain, is not that I sit and talk with them like I am here talking to you; but I can sense what they want to say - it's an intuitive communication, a feeling, like telepathic, the communication happens in lots of different ways and I put into words what I am receiving so that the owners can help their animals in the best possible way."

"Wow, that is amazing, can you take me one day, so I can watch you, do it?"

"Yes, I am going to a farm tomorrow afternoon, and there you can see how it works. There are lots of racehorse breeders here in Chile as in the UK there are many racecourses and the owners will do anything for their thoroughbreds, and they pay me really well but for me, it's not about the money, but it gives me real satisfaction to help animals as much as I can".

Margarita stood up. "We better go to bed now; otherwise I won't be able to even talk to you tomorrow let alone a horse."

I went back to my room and thought I wouldn't be able to sleep, but as soon as my head touched the pillow, I dozed off.

In the afternoon we set off and Margarita started driving along in one of the most scenic roads I had ever seen, cruising along a gorge flanked by mountains on both sides.

"The roads here are fantastic, Chile doesn't seem like a third-world country to me."

"Chile has its problems, but there isn't extreme poverty like in most third-world countries; I would rate it as a second-world country."

We then left the main road and joined a country lane.

"This is the reason I have a 4x4, when the weather is bad these roads are not fit for purpose."

We drove for another 20 minutes until we reached a beautiful ranch, surrounded by huge tall trees; and a young tall slim man came to greet us. He was wearing jeans and a hat and looked very much like an elegant Western cowboy.

"Hello, Margarita I am so glad you could come here today, as you had said you had a visitor and maybe you wouldn't be able to come."

"Hello Raúl, this is my friend Gaby, she arrived yesterday from London, and she wants to experience what I do, I hope you don't mind me bringing her along?"

"Not at all, let go to the stables and I show you the horse I need you to see."

We walked into a very large stable, very clean and bright, a few horses showed their faces as we walk along the pathway.

"The horse we are going to see is a stallion, I've owned him since he was three, and he is now twenty-five, he is a thoroughbred," Raúl said as he slid open the door where the horse was; there stood the most beautiful white stallion. "Don't worry, he is very sweet, he won't harm us, we can go in and say hello, his name is Carmelo, and I don't want to say much about him as I don't really want to give away anything."

Margarita went inside the stable and I just stood outside watching. She put her hand on the horse's neck, and started caressing him softly; he moved his head and started licking her hand.

"He is such a nice guy, I first let him smell me and touch me, and let him get more comfortable with me; the first thing he wants to say is that if he can stay here with you, he is worried about it because there are some horses that leave and go to other stables and as he is not that young anymore, he is worried you will send him away and he wants a reassurance that he can stay."

"Yes, he will stay here with me forever, you can tell him that." Raúl said in a very reassuring tone.

"That is why he hasn't been eating well lately because there were some people that came here the other day and asked if they could buy him, and you will be surprised what animals can hear, and he heard that."

"Oh, wow yes, they did, but I can never sell Carmelo, he is my horse, we still compete in Horse Trials and will do it for as long as he is willing and capable of doing so, I thought he wanted to give up as he hasn't been eating much and that is why I called you."

"He has given me a sigh of relief, and he says he really wants to go on competing with you", said Margarita in a very soft voice so as not to upset Carmelo.

"Well, I am also feeling relieved and tell him I will never send him away or get rid of him, we have gone through many upheavals together and as much as I have trained him, he has taught me many things too, but tell him, that I will also train some other horses and compete with them too, but he should never feel jealous, as he will always be my horse." Raúl said it almost choking as Carmelo was nodding as if he understood what he just said, and I could feel tears rolling down my cheeks I had never witnessed such an amazing communication between a man and his horse, and all made possible by Margarita.

We went out of the stables and I walked just behind them as I wanted to give Margarita and Raúl some space, I could hear them talking about other animal and what Raúl could do for them.

We got back in the 4x4 and headed back to Santiago.

"Margarita, that was one of the most remarkable things I have ever witnessed, can anyone talk to animals like you do?"

"I am sure anyone can do it, in fact, all animal lovers do it unconsciously, I remember watching my Mum talking to her favourite cocker spaniel Katia, and she would just sit there in front of my Mum begging her to take her out for a walk, and my Mum would "know" what the dog wanted and would just stand up and get her lead and the dog would bark and wag her tail, saying "thank you". All animal owners have a certain level of communication with their pets even though they are not actually aware that they are talking to them. Animals are far more intelligent than people give them credit for, and they are very aware of the owner's feelings, when someone is sad or ill, they can sense it, and they would go and sit close to their owner trying to comfort them. Cats are great healers, and a dog will give his life to see his owner happy."

"Maybe when I get back home, I will get myself a pet, probably a cat; I like their independent and aloof attitude."

"I couldn't live without animals around me, besides Diego and Frida, I also have a black cat called Shakira, she will come out and greet you when you least expect it, so don't be afraid."

We stopped at a restaurant to have some dinner; Margarita ordered two seafood empanadas and two cheese ones. When they arrived, they were huge empanadas.

"I don't think I can eat all that, I will have to book an extra seat on the flight back if I eat too much during my holidays" I said laughing.

We talked and joked for a while. I felt as if I had known Margarita all my life, it's amazing how you get that feeling with some people, there is that instant connection, and some that when you meet them you instantly reject.

I mention that to Margarita:

"Animals are very good at that, they can pick up the energy of a person immediately, and that is why I never trust a person if my dogs bark at them, I know then they are not trustworthy."

I kept staring and Margarita, she had a beautiful complexion and she wasn't wearing any makeup at all.

"Can I ask you what face cream you use? Your skin looks amazing."

"This is top secret, here we all use organic Chilean Rosehip Oil, it is the best in the world. We can go and buy some tomorrow as I have to buy some for Lucia, I used to send her some by mail but the regulations have changed and now you just can't send any liquids, and it's impossible to just send oil by airmail."

"I better fill my luggage with tons of it, your skin is amazing and so is Lucia's."

We set again in the 4x4 towards Margarita's home and she then asked me:

"What would you like to do during the next few days, I have taken a week off work but I rather do what you would like to see the most. I only went to see Raúl today as you showed some interest in what I do, but I have told my clients to wait unless it's urgent."

"What are my options as you know I only have a week and Chile is such a big country?"

"Well, we can go and visit the Colchagua Valley; it's the centre of wine production in Chile. There are several wineries in the valley that offer tours with amazing wine tasting, maybe go to the Santa Cruz Vineyard as is one of the most symbolic in the area. A cable car takes you to the top of the Chamán Hill in the evening, where you can see constellations at the observatory they have there. Chile has a very clear sky and some of the biggest observatories in the world are here; or; we can take the costal route up north, we can go first to Viña del Mar, a beautiful city where the famous international song contest takes place, unfortunately there are only a few old buildings still remain after multiple <u>earthquakes</u> that have destroyed most of the old areas of the city and it's now very modern with lots of skyscrapers. We can then go to La Serena, in the north, is a very old city and it has beautiful beaches, and then go to the Atacama Desert where the James Bond film Quantum of Solace was filmed, there, we can stay in the award-winning hotel The Paranal Residencia that you can see in the film, and visit the

Cerro Paranal Observatory that is one of the largest in the country. South is green, and north is dessert," said Margarita very enthusiastically.

"Oh, dear how can I choose, everything sounds absolutely amazing; I think I will have to flip a coin." I took a coin out of my bag and said; "Heads north, Tails vineyards." I flipped the coin up in the air and it flew out the window of the 4x4.

"Not even the coin could make up its mind, we better sleep on it.", I said laughing out loud.

As soon as we arrived home my mobile started ringing nonstop.

"Looks like London is on fire." said Margarita, looking at my phone.

"That is what happens when you are without internet for a whole day, but I do enjoy disconnecting from everyone, it's quite liberating and it does help me reconnect with myself. It happened a lot when I was travelling around the Himalayas, and since then, when I travel, I don't make any effort to purchase any SIM cards or get connected but just when it's available and the minimum time possible." I said it quite enthusiastically.

"I should give it a try as I don't seem to get away from the damned phone not even when I go to the toilet."

I went to my bedroom and started looking at my messages, there was one from George; "All is well, enjoy yourself" and one long one from Linda; "I told the boys, and besides being very surprised and asking who the father was, they seemed quite happy and offered me all their support but I haven't managed to tell Tom yet, although he suspects there is something going on, as I have been avoiding him as much as I can. He has asked me out to dinner on Thursday, and somehow, I will have to find some courage and tell him there and then, I can't delay it anymore, I will keep you posted."

"Dear Linda, you know you can count on me for anything, I will help you in any way you want me too, so don't worry about what Tom might say, you can always come and work for me at the centre, so please don't worry about money either, will sort something good for you and the baby. Changing subject, I'm having a good time after a never-ending flight, I really like it here, I am amazed to see how developed Chile is, I wasn't expecting this, very pleasantly surprised, Lucia's sister is amazing, she is an animal communicator, it's incredible I will tell you all about it when I get back, will have to skip the Prosecco but we can have a pyjama party. Love you."

As soon as I turned my phone off, Margarita came running to my bedroom.

"We are going North, will have to skip the vineyards, I have a client that has called me urgently as one of his dogs has turned quite violent and he wants me to take a look, and as he lives quite near La Serena we can stay there and then drive to the Atacama Desert."

"Good, I like it when things work out by themselves; it means that it was meant to be. When do we leave?"

"Early tomorrow morning, so pack a small bag for about 3 to 4 days."

"I will go to bed now; I will skip dinner as we had such a big lunch."

I gave Margarita a kiss and went to bed, but as I couldn't go to sleep I tried meditating, counting sheep, you name it, I tried it and just when I was dozing off; Margarita knocked at the door.

"Time to go, Gaby," she opened the door and handed me a cup of coffee. "You look terrible, did you sleep OK?"

"Not exactly, I think I ran a full marathon turning and tossing in bed."

"That is called jetlag; you can sleep in the car as it is quite a long drive to the client's ranch."

We set off in the 4x4 and before we even left Santiago, I was gone.

"Time to wake up, sleeping beauty, we are nearly there." Margarita said, shaking my legs; "Here, drink some water; we are about 10 minutes away."

"Wow, what time is it?"

"Quarter to one."

"I've been asleep all morning and missed all the scenery?"

"Don't worry you can see it all on the way back."

We arrived at another very large ranch that looked more like a sheep farm, a couple came to greet us this time.

"Margarita, so glad you could come, please get your bags, we have prepared a room for you and your friend, is the least we can do for you for coming all this way," said a very pretty middle aged woman with a ponytail. She extended her hand to greet me.

"Welcome Gaby, I hope you had a good journey, I'm Isabel and this is my husband Felipe, come, follow me and I will show you to your room.

We walked along a long corridor and right at the end, Isabel opened the door that led to a very large bedroom, and it had a Scandinavian look, with a large fireplace and sheepskin rugs beside each bed.

"I hope you are comfortable here, there is a large bathroom across the corridor. I hope you don't mind."

"Everything looks great, thanks," said Margarita. But, now take me to see the dog."

We all walked out into a large barn and inside there was a cage and in it, a very large black Rottweiler.

"His name is Bonzo", said Felipe, "He used to be my favourite dog, the most trusted and loyal and now I can't even get close to him and I don't know why."

As soon as we opened the door he started barking and growling, but as soon as Margarita got closer, he calmed down. She stayed there staring at him and Bonzo stared back, we all stood there quietly just watching.

"He is telling me, that there is a new foreman that has been very violent towards him and that he is putting something in his food that is making him behave like this, but he doesn't really mean to be aggressive and least of all towards you."

"That must be the new guy, Luis, I've never liked the way he looks at me," said Isabel "He gives me the creeps."

"He is telling me that he is not a nice guy and that he wants to create chaos in the farm so he can control it. He has overheard him talking to other men in the evenings.

Felipe immediately changed the water and the food in Bonzo's cage and got close to him and stroked him. "Sorry my friend, I will make it up to you." Bonzo started howling.

"He is feeling very pleased that he has been able to let you know the truth of what's going in the farm and that if you let him out the cage, he will chase Luis and his associates out of the farm."

"That would be great fun to watch but we don't want those bastards close to you ever again, this is something I have to do myself."

Felipe burst out of the barn and a minute later we heard him shouting at Luis telling to leave and never to come back.

Once he had left, Felipe came back to the barn. Bonzo was rather pleased with himself and said he wanted to have a long sleep as the substance that Luis had been giving him didn't let him relax and he was very tired. He put a paw over Margarita's hand through the cage, thanking her.

Felipe asked us to go to the house and he was going to check Luis's office to see if he could find any traces of any substances there.

"We better go and get something to eat, after all the events I am very hungry and I bet you, ladies must be very hungry too," said Isabel.

Margarita and I looked at each other, we had only had just that one cup of coffee before we set of from Santiago and we were famished.

"But, let's open a bottle of wine first; I think we deserve a large glass, red or white?"

As we were sitting by the table, Felipe walked holding a couple of bags with powder inside them.

"Margarita, I don't know how to thank you for what you just did, not only did you save Bonzo from being put down, but you saved my home and my business and my life. I'm taking these bags to be examined, God knows what they are."

"Just make sure that you report Luis to the authorities, we don't want another dog going through what Bonzo had to endure."

We stayed talking and drinking in the veranda for quite a long time and we set off early next morning towards the desert. Felipe and Isabel waved us goodbye, and it was lovely to see a relaxed and well behaved Bonzo sitting proudly next to his owner.

"Where to?" I asked Margarita.

"Well, we are going to spend the next two nights at the Paranal Residencia that I told you about yesterday, it is very expensive and difficult to get a room, but Felipe wanted to treats us and he paid for the whole stay, all inclusive, thanks to Bonzo!"

"No thanks to Bonzo, thanks to you, you were amazing, I am gobsmacked."

Margarita just smiled, "I love what I do, there is no better feeling for me than to give a voice to animals and close the gap between a man and his pet."

The drive to Cerro Paranal was very long and tiring, I was very grateful to Margarita as I couldn't bring myself to drive on the other side of the road; the scenery was amazing and ever changing but the climb to the hotel was quite something, red mountains that reminded me a bit of the Grand Canyon, and when we were finally approaching our destination, all I could see was a very large white dome and some very rustic copper buildings that blended quite seamless with the landscape. But when you step into the buildings you enter this most amazing huge indoor garden with a very large swimming pool, surrounded by very tall palm trees.

"Goodness, gracious, wow! This is certainly an oasis in the middle of the dessert." I couldn't stop looking at the whole thing; I just wanted to take it all in.

We were then shown to our bedrooms; they were quite modest in comparison with the dramatic entrance to the hotel.

"I will take a shower and then I will go to the garden area, I don't want to go to sleep and mess up my sleeping pattern, now that my brain has finally adapted to Chilean time."

"I will probably do the same, just relaxing around the pool until dinner time would be just what the doctor ordered."

"And, two glasses of Prosecco," I winked at her.

We looked very refreshed and relaxed when we stepped into the garden area, we sat there and before we could order anything the waiter brought us two glasses of champagne.

"From the gentleman over there," he said pointing at a man sitting by himself in one of the tables.

We lifted our glasses and before we could drink the champagne, he was sitting right next to us.

What are two beautiful ladies doing here is such a remote place on earth, unless you are astronomers?" he said in a very strong Scottish accent, he had ginger hair and freckles but he was rather cute.

"And what is a Scotsman doing such a long way from home?" I retorted.

"You see, ladies, the Cerro Paranal Observatory belongs to a European Consortium, so all of us here come from afar, and don't tell me you came all the way here just for the ride?"

Margarita and I looked at each other and we burst out laughing, we didn't have a clue what we were doing there.

"Did I say something funny?" he asked quite surprised.

"No, we just realized that we don't exactly know what we are doing here", said Margarita, in a very sweet tone of voice, the same tone she uses when communicating with animals, and the Scotsman was totally smitten.

"What is your name?" she asked him.

"I'm Roger but everyone here calls me Scott."

"I'm Margarita and I am showing my friend Gaby around Chile."

"This is definitely not on the tourist agenda of places to visit in Chile. Let's have dinner and then I can take you up to the Observatory."

"Tonight?" I asked him.

"Well, yes, observatories are best seen during the night, stargazing doesn't happen during the day, we do have day tours but if you want to see the telescopes in action, it is best if we go at night, we have one of the top telescopes in the world here at Paranal and it's one of the very best astronomical observation sites around the globe, and as you haven't got a clue what you are doing here, I will show you what I am doing here." Scott said in a rather proud tone of voice.

We talked just about everything over dinner, he asked me about the UK but, his interest and stargazing evolved around Margarita. Scott later took us to the Observatory and the closer we got to the site, the immensity of it all just hit me, we were like midgets standing next to the buildings that house the telescopes, and it all looks like a place more suitable in a Star Wars film that on planet earth. Everyone seemed to know Scott and he looked rather pleased to be seen walking around with two beautiful ladies. He took us to see the Very Large Telescope.

"This is the largest telescope in Paranal; you can just about see anything in the vast Universe."

"Do you come across UFOs?" I asked him, and I told him about my experiences in Glastonbury with Luis Fernando.

"We do see a lot of unexplained objects, but I am more interested in finding a new galaxy, a new star that I can name maybe after one of you", he said looking directly at Margarita.

We then took a look at the stars using the telescope and that made me realize that planet Earth is just a tiny speck in the vastness of the universe and chances that we are the only inhabited planet are very slim.

We spent the next two days driving around the area and sitting by the pool, mostly with Scott, that was now totally ignoring me and all eyes were focused on Margarita.

We said goodbye and somehow I thought that this was not the last time Margarita was going to see Scott.

On the way back, we stopped at La Serena just to break the journey, and we spent the day walking around this beautiful old town and lying by the beach.

Margarita then said, "I've received a text message from Raúl, he won a national trial with Carmelo and he is very happy, as they are back on top form."

"I still can't get my head round what you do, what a beautiful gift."

"The sooner that us humans realize that animals are our equals and that they do have a purpose here on earth too and that we all can walk hand in hand on this earth looking after each other, the sooner that this planet will be a better place for all of us to live in."

Back at home in Santiago I connected to the internet, I wanted to hear from Linda and her dinner with Tom.

"Dear Gaby, I am hiding in your flat, Tom wasn't happy at me being pregnant, and all he wants is for me to have an abortion, maybe that is the best way for everyone, but deep down I would really like to have this baby."

"Dear Linda, do what your heart wants, and what you feel is right for you, we can bring this baby up between us. I would love to be a standby Mum, love you lots, Gaby."

I turned my phone off and just wished I could be there for her during these difficult times.

In Santiago, Margarita took me the Central Market, Santiago's most famous market. Located in the city centre, this wrought-iron building is considered a historical landmark where we had the best seafood I've ever tried in my life. We visited a few other places and I was amazed at how beautiful Santiago was and it left a very good impression in my heart, mainly due to Margarita's hospitality.

Saying goodbye at the airport was hard, we had formed such a strong bond in the short time we spent together and I made her promised she would come and visit me and her sister in London.

Bolivia

Landing in La Paz was a far cry from landing in Santiago. The airport was in absolute chaos, besides feeling totally dizzy due to the altitude, La Paz is the highest city in the world and the airport is located in El Alto that is even higher, around 4.000 meters above sea level. There in a corner, as I was waiting for my luggage to appear, stood an Indian lady dressed in the most beautiful attire with a top black hat white blouse and a black skirt, with lots of colourful necklaces; she was offering coca tea. "It's good for altitude sickness", she said. As she handed me a cup, I imagined being offered coca tea on arrival at Heathrow.

When I finally retrieved my luggage and stepped out of the door, Luis Fernando was waiting for me with his girlfriend. The most beautiful woman I had ever seen, she looked like a model, very slim with shoulder length hair and deep brown eyes. No wonder Luis Fernando wasn't interested in anybody else whilst on his journeys.

"Welcome to La Paz, this is Anita, my fiancée; did you have a good flight?"

"The flight was alright but I'm feeling really odd, I'm so sorry I don't seem to think straight."

Anita held me by my waist and Luis Fernando carried my luggage.

"Como on, let's get you home so you can lie down for a while, it takes some time to get used to this altitude", said Anita in a very soft voice but with a slight accent.

"Where are you from?" I asked her.

"I'm Italian."

"How on earth did you end here in La Paz?"

"It's a long story, when you are feeling better I will tell you how I ended up here with Luis Fernando."

As we were walking towards the car, I could see the Andes close by and the Illimani Mountain, the highest in this part of the Andes, with its magnificent snowed peak that looked so near that it seemed that you could almost touch them. Luis Fernando's car was a large jeep.

As we started driving from the Alto towards La Paz, I could see why Luis Fernando needed a jeep. The roads were treacherous and very congested with street sellers flanking both sides, but the vistas were magnificent, as we approached a point where you could see La Paz down in a valley surrounded by mountains and there on the side there is a cable car that joins the Alto with La Paz:

"I don't think I will be using the cable car; it looks quite scary" I said making a panicking face.

"No need to be frightened, you in Europe have underground trains, here we use cable cars as it's the only way to have public transport that is quick and safe, I can assure it's a safer way to travel than on the roads here."

And I soon found out what he meant when we started plunging through a very narrow road, with buses coming towards us and nearly missing us on every curve, I had to close my eyes, it was even worse than in India, as there was heavy traffic and nobody respected any of the road signs. Luis Fernando was a very good driver and obviously had a lot of experience negotiating these roads and we finally arrived at his house; a magnificent white modern building set high in the mountains. We walked into the house which it was very tastefully decorated with some traditional furniture and a few Pre-Columbian ornaments dotted around the house, but it really was all about the vistas. What a view! I was shown to my bedroom as I needed to lie down, and soon fell asleep. In mid-afternoon Anita came with some more coca tea and she gently touched me.

"I think is better if you wake up now, otherwise you are going to mess up your sleeping pattern", she said in her soft voice.

"Oh, dear I can't have that again, it took me a long time to adjust to Chilean time", I said getting quickly out of bed, but I soon had to sit down as the dizziness came straight back."

"Take it easy,"said Anita and then I remembered I had some of the tablets my German friend Wagner had given me for the altitude in the Himalayas and I quickly took one of them and after a couple of hours I was back to normal.

"What are those tablets?" Luis Fernando asked.

"A friend of mine gave them to me in the Himalayas, they are the tablets given to those who climb Mount Everest and they are wonderful, but I don't really know the name as they are German."

"Better ask your friend as I could give some to everyone when they arrive here in La Paz."

We sat at the table to have dinner and Anita said:

"Now I can tell you all about how Luis Fernando and I met. In 2010, I was studying and practicing my yoga and also working on lucid dreams. I was receiving very important information regarding my life at the time, and one evening, I was taken to a spaceship and the commander of the ship was monitoring me with a tool because he was making sure that I was going to remember the experience and that I could sustain myself there, because the vibration was very high, as what usually happens in these circumstances is that you tend to forget or suffer amnesia. I realized where I was, and I tried to take notice of all that was happening around me so I could remember everything, I then heard a crew member calling me AKIRA, a name that sounded very familiar and I answered to that name throughout this whole experience. When I met Luis Fernando I found out that this is what they refer to as cosmic name. Later on, at the beginning of 2011, I had a dream where a guide told me that I came from Lemuria, and at the time I didn't really know what this meant, so when I woke up I immediately wrote it down and I googled it, and the first thing that came up was Mount Shasta, the city of Telos and the name of Luis Fernando Mostajo. I wrote down his name but I set it aside as I was more interested in studying about Lemuria, but later on I noticed that he was going to give a talk in a seminar in Mount Shasta in September 2011 and I decided to go. I bought the ticket and I got in touch with Luis Fernando and I told him everything about my dream and that I needed to go, as I was researching my Lemurian origins, but unfortunately Luis Fernando couldn't go, because he had some problems with his construction company in Bolivia but he put me in touch with his friends in San Francisco, and they picked me up at the airport and took me to Mount Shasta, where I had an amazing experience. At the time I was ending a relationship and when I was in Mount Shasta I did a ritual under the new moon, where I sent to the universe a list of things that I wanted for my life, and one of them was, that if there was going to be a new man in my future, he had to be Lemurian. Afterwards we went to the house of Raúl Domínguez, who usually organizes things for Luis Fernando there, and I saw a picture of them both and I thought to myself, that he was rather handsome. Back home in Italy the date 11:11 came to my mind and that I should be in the Isla del Sol in Lake Titicaca as it was directly linked to Mount Shasta, I was looking to see if there were any events I could attend there, and was also a bit nervous and reluctant as traveling on my own to an island in the middle of this lake; was not the same as traveling to California, so I asked Luis Fernando, and he said there wasn't anything. I kept going on with my life as usual and after a couple of days I asked my guides that if I really needed to be there, they had to help me out, and I took a deep breath and right at that moment I received a message from Luis Fernando, saying that there were no official events, but that if I wanted to go, he could pick me up at the airport and help me on my way to the island. I took this as a sign that I had to go, so I went. I arrived at a very chaotic airport in La Paz at 3 am; I was very tired and disoriented. Once I collected my luggage, I went out through the international arrivals doors and there in the distance I noticed him, and he also noticed me and he stood up and started walking towards me, and there and then I heard a clear voice in my head that said: "He is the love of your Life." I had to sit down due to the altitude and the lack of oxygen and was feeling very confused and set aside what I had just heard. We met, and I eventually got into Luis Fernando's car and I could feel the vibration rising and felt this instant energetic connection. He took me to his house, and I won't mention exactly what happened but we both started to have very strong feelings for each other and one thing led to another and we ended up together in Isla del Sol on the 11:11. From then on, I went travelling by myself around Peru, but we kept in touch and soon after, we met in Barcelona at an UFO world conference and I went back to Bolivia with him and then I remember the voice in my head: "He is the love of your life" and the rest is history."

"Wow, what a beautiful story, I hope one day I meet the love of my life too and have such an amazing life as you two have."

When we finished our dinner, we walked outside the house just to admire the view and the stars; I told them all about my time at the Cerro Paranal Observatory.

"Such a beautiful Universe, I just wondered how many planets are inhabited, there must be millions of different species and races out there, I can't begin to think what is going to happen once they start landing and finally show up; if we are racist here on planet earth just with a few differences in colour and feature variations, what are we going to do with such a range of races and cultures?"

"That is one of the reasons they haven't started landing, we are not ready for that yet, but they will be starting to show themselves a bit more."

"Look," said Luis Fernando pointing at the sky at two very bright lights crossing the sky at an unbelieve speed and very close to each other.

"They must have heard you," I said smiling.

"They are just letting us know they are there."

I was amazed at how the spaceships seemed to follow Luis Fernando. It was a fantastic experience.

"Right, we better go to bed, it's getting cold out here and tomorrow we are going to the Pre-Columbian city of Tiwanaku," said Anita.

I went back to my room and as I had slept for such a long time I couldn't close my eyes. I looked at my emails and answered a few, and then a WhatsApp message from Linda appeared on my screen:

"Hi Gaby, hope you are enjoying Bolivia and meeting up with Luis Fernando again, and please don't go in a spaceship to another planet, I need you here on planet earth, it's bad enough that you are so far away right now, so please don't run away any further."

"Hello Linda, just arrived today, lovely to see Luis Fernando again, and meeting his fiancée, she is beautiful inside and out. What are you doing up so early, it must be 4am UK time?"

"Well, it's difficult to sleep nowadays, I am still at yours, I think Tom is going crazy on his own at the office, and not knowing where on earth I am, he keeps sending me messages day and night."

"Turn the phone off, or block him for a while, that will make him even crazier. Whatever you do, don't give in."

"I think he is more worried about his clients and managing the office on his own that me being pregnant."

"Serves him right, if anything that company should be in both your names, you are more a manager than his PA. Keep me updated, we better go to sleep, I have an early start tomorrow."

"Sweet dreams, Linda".

I fell asleep worrying about Linda, hoping Tom would come round and realize what an amazing woman Linda is.

Early next morning, Anita came into my bedroom with a cup of coffee.

"I am going to meditate before we set off, would you like to join me?"

We went into a small room that had a very relaxing atmosphere. Anita lit some incense and guided me in a beautiful meditation. She looked very much like an angel on earth while she was meditating, a special soul, one of those who have come to this earth to help raise the vibration as I could feel mine right there in that moment going through the roof. When she finally brought me back, she gave me a big smile.

"We better go and find Luis Fernando." We went down to the entrance of the house and he was waiting for us in the jeep.

"Good morning, ladies, ready for today's adventure?"

"Can't wait!" I said, as I was really excited to be going to Tiwanaku, the oldest Pre-Columbian city in Latin America.

Luis Fernando drove past the old city centre of La Paz and its very beautiful colonial buildings, the streets were crowded and there were lots of Indians walking around with their very colourful outfits. It was as I had envisaged all Latin American countries to be. We then started climbing to the Alto and when we reached up there and were driving through the main road, I started noticing these iconic and highly colourful buildings.

"Wow, I love those buildings, what are they?" I asked Luis Fernando.

"Those are neo-Andean constructions created by **Freddy Mamani,** a self-taught architect that comes from an Aymara indigenous family. He takes his inspiration from their textiles and ceramics, and has transformed the face of El Alto and now people come from all over the world just to admire his architecture."

"They are amazing; I have never seen anything like it."

We started driving outside the city and into the countryside beautiful panoramic view of the Andes, the road was quite treacherous so I just kept my focus on the view. At one point we could see Lake Titicaca, the highest lake on earth.

"We are going to visit the Lake another day when we go and visit the external retreat at "Wiñaymarka", a place I built on the shores of the lake. I will tell you all about it when we go there the days after tomorrow."

"So many places to see here in Bolivia, what and amazing country!"

"This a very special place and it's not a coincidence that I was born here. During thousands of years the cosmic energy used to concentrate in the magical and mythical mountains of Tibet, but after WWII, this masculine energy started to transfer here to America in its feminine aspect, all along the Andes going all the way up to Mount Shasta, but has its centre here in Lake Titicaca. The planet is now moving towards a more balanced feminine and masculine era, and as you know we have seven chakras and Planet Earth also has these seven chakras all connected by ley lines that move the energy of the planet and they are mostly felt in these amazing highly vibrational energetic locations. The Root Chakra is situated in Mount Shasta, in California, an active volcano; it's a very spiritual place for North American tribes. The Root Chakra is responsible for helping energy move upwards, which is exactly what a volcano does when it erupts. The Sacral Chakra is located here in Lake Titicaca and is believed to be the womb of the planet and encompasses both masculine and feminine energies, as two ley lines, cross at this point that represents our feminine and masculine, a truly sacred place for all the indigenous tribes that live around it. The Solar Plexus Chakra, placed in Uluru & Kata Tjuta in Australia is associated with self-confidence, personal power, self-worth, and willpower. The Heart Chakra, as you know Gaby, is in Glastonbury and is associated with the emotions of love, compassion, and understanding, something the Earth needs a lot of right now and going to this place and then coming here as you and I have done, will help move this energy around. The Throat Chakra situated in the Pyramids of Giza and Mount Sinai in Egypt, and the Mount of Olives in Jerusalem, Israel. It's believed that these three locations connect to make up the Throat Chakra which governs our voice, our truth and self-expression. The Pyramids of Egypt are unique too as this isn't a spot where ley lines intersect, but it is one of Earth's energy vortexes. The Third Eye is a Floating Chakra and the only one that can move and is currently also positioned in Glastonbury. The Third Eye is linked with our intuition, hence the importance of going to Glastonbury right now, the vibration there is extremely high and finally the Crown Chakra, located in Mount Kailash in Tibet, known as the "roof of the world". It is connected to enlightenment, and connections with the spirit world, one of the most sacred mountains in the Himalayas, and close to where the Dalai Lama lives. The Tibetan monks do so much for the energy of the planet; I don't know what would happen to Earth if it wasn't for them."

"I know, I've been there, and thanks for all this information I will definitely go more often to Glastonbury when I get back home, such an amazing place and I should take more advantage of it living so close to it."

"But now we are arriving at the special city of Tiwanaku," said Anita. She had been very quiet throughout this whole journey, just listening to the conversation.

We entered a long road until we reached the site. It was very sunny and felt quite warm, I was very surprised being so high up in the mountains.

"Better use a lot of sun cream as you can easily get sunstroke here, and here, put on this hat." Anita handed me a big cowboy hat and I felt like Butch Cassidy arriving in Bolivia.

Tiwanaku is an ancient civilisation which disappeared long before the Incas, and has these incredible structures aligned with the stars and perfectly carved temples, built more than 10.000 years BC. We started walking around the ruins and were surprised to see such a vast place; the precision of all the buildings is still an enigma that baffles everyone that visits this site.

"This area of the archaeological complex is very important. It is known as "Puma Punku"; even the scholars consider this area as technology not built by humans."

"Luis Fernando, this place is surely proof that extra-terrestrials have visited Earth, I can't see any other explanation for this place being here."

He looked at me and smiled: "I'm glad you figured this one out by yourself, I am going to show you the biggest proof we have here of extra-terrestrial intervention."

We continued walking and then Luis Fernando pointed out an area.

"This here is the pyramid of Akapana and that one there," Luis Fernando said pointing at a stone portal, "is the famous Puerta del Sol, that was built perfectly aligned with the sun movements, and during the solstice the first rays of the sun raise right in the middle of it. Further along we reached the main courtyard that is partially submerged decorated all around it with faces from different cultures around the world and there amongst those faces there is one of an extra-terrestrial, with its big elongated ayes. Luis Fernando pointed at this carved face and just looked at me.

"Is there any doubt now?" He also pointed at the features of some of the other faces, some had Tibetan features and some looked like African people. How could they have seen all these other civilizations if they couldn't fly? Tiwanaku is nearly 4.000 meters above sea level and very far from any coastline, and to bring any of these stones up here and cut and build it all with such precision, even before the wheel was invented is absolutely impossible, they also had such a remarkable knowledge of astronomy and solar alignments and they had such a sophisticated irrigation system that is well beyond anything that could have been built by anyone other than extra-terrestrials." Luis Fernando said very convincingly.

I walked around Tiwanaku and saw many similarities with Stonehenge and the pyramids of Egypt, and many other highly sophisticated stone buildings dotted around the world. Maybe Luis Fernando was right, and we had probably been visited by ETs throughout our history and they had helped build all these amazing places.

We went to the museum which houses some huge statues and ceramics and ornaments that had been found around the area, but what really blew me away was the elongated human skulls that clearly pointed to an extra-terrestrial influence, and it all just made me wondered how Tiwanaku came to be.

On our way back to La Paz we stopped to have some dinner and Luis Fernando explained to me more about this place.

"Tiwanaku is within a very important planetary ley line network, it's located in the vortex of the cosmic energy in its feminine aspect, a positive and negative polarity that all things in creation have."

"The Lemurian civilization, considered today as the cradle of our human civilization established here in Tiwanaku a solar activation initiation centre. This solar activation made it possible to receive cosmic information and also to get in synchronicity and in harmony with the forces of nature through the centre of mother earth. So, when we come to this area that is now in ruins but energetically very active, we have the possibility of rearranging our physical structure into a new photonic frequency of light and that is what the masters are doing now a days here in this initiation temple known as Tiwanaku, that also holds the most fabulous and fantastic power tool: the "Solar Disk." This disk has the ability to stabilize the forces of nature and can also enable us to integrate in a harmonious and balanced way these forces permitting us to be co-creators of our new reality. When humanity is ready, this disk will be revealed to all."

"Nowadays only ten per cent of the archaeological site of Tiwanaku has been unearthed, there are thermo-satellite photos and analysis that show that there are many constructions all around this area, there is a lot of investment needed here because as you can see it's all in ruins."

"I saw a BBC documentary about the archaeological site at Tikal and they showed infra-red photos of the area that exposed many buildings in the Central American jungles waiting to be discovered," I said to Luis Fernando.

"Yes, there are so many areas around the Earth that still hold so much information, as in the poles, the dessert, the Amazon jungle, and the oceans. They all safeguard treasures and mysteries still waiting to be exposed and I am sure that one day they will all be revealed," Luis Fernando said it as he stood up and we all walked back to the jeep.

When we arrived back home, I just crushed into my bed and fell asleep in two seconds as I was very tired.

The next day after my meditation with Anita; we set out to a place called El Valle de la Luna or Valley of the Moon; the journey to this place was place very pleasant and relaxed and close to La Paz. As soon as we walked into the complex, I truly felt like we had landed on the moon, this place is a labyrinth of spires and canyons created from sandstone and clay in a variation of beige, brown and red tones, dotted around these formations are several cacti, as it is the only plant that can grow is such a dry landscape.

Anita pointed out to a particular variety: "That one there is the San Pedro variety that has hallucinogenic properties and the Andean indigenous people use them when they connect with Pachamama."

"Have you ever tried them?" I asked her.

"No, I connect through meditation I don't need hallucinogens to get any spiritual connections but the Shamans have been using them for ages, and if you ever want to try some, you have to do it with a good Shaman, there are many fakes around, preying on tourist like you, so be very careful, especially as you are travelling to Peru."

On the way back to their house I asked Luis Fernando to drop me in La Paz, I wanted to walk around the town centre.

"Be very careful with your handbag and don't accept anything from anyone, and call me when you finish, I will come and pick you up", he sounded more like my father than a friend.

I stepped out of the jeep close to the cathedral, one of the largest cathedrals I have ever seen, a very impressive building. I went inside and started walking around it and as I was looking at the celling and not where I was going, I accidentally bumped into a guy.

"I am so sorry," I said to him, "I didn't mean to."

"Oh, you are English? Love your accent."

I blushed. "Yes, I am from London, and again I am very sorry."

"Don't be sorry, this is an impressive building, one is easily distracted." He offered me his hand; "I am Erik, from Toronto."

He was tall, with dark long hair drawn back in a ponytail, was wearing a pair of scruffy jeans and hiking boots, but underneath all that he was rather handsome. We started talking and he mentioned that he had been travelling from Brazil to Argentina and now Bolivia, and was intending to go all the way to Colombia before heading home to Canada. I told him I was going to Peru and then going back home to England.

"Where are you going now?"

"I really don't know, my friends dropped me here and I was just going to walk around the city centre before calling them to pick me up."

"Would you like to go to the Witches' Market, apparently it is really good, full of artefacts and magic mushrooms and potions?"

I thought about what Anita had said to be weary of fake Shamans, but he looked rather harmless and he was good-looking.

"Yes, why not, is it far from here?"

He took a Lonely Planet guidebook out of his pocket and read: "It says here that we have to take the bus number 44 and it's about a 20 minutes' drive to the market."

Number 44 my favourite angel number, I immediately felt quite relaxed, as that was always a sign that I was on the right track. We had to wait for quite a while for the bus and when it finally arrived it was packed, we managed to find some seats a row apart and both sitting next to and Indian lady.

"Please take my photo sitting next to this lovely lady, my Mum would love to see me here, she loves this culture, and she was the one that encouraged me to travel around South America. I wanted to go to Thailand but she persuaded me to come here instead." He handed me his mobile phone and when the lady saw that I was taking her picture, she gave him a big hug and a huge smile and I took a beautiful picture of both of them. Erik gave her a few dollars and she was very happy.

When we arrived at the Market it was an amazing display of stalls with colourful artefacts and people trying to sell you anything you could think of, it was very crowded so I held to Erik for dear life. He laughed at me.

"Don't worry, I won't let anything happen to you and as I already survived travelling along the North Yungas Road, the most dangerous road in the world where buses and trucks often go tumbling down the Andes off its rather precarious edge; I am sure I can survive one afternoon in this market," he said with a beautiful big smile.

I still held very tightly to him and I think he was rather enjoying me being so close to him. We were offered all sorts of potions and Ayahuasca experiences with "trusted" Shamans and I then told him what Anita had said to me.

We later left the market and walked around La Paz, such a busy city but I loved all the hustle and bustle of the place. We had a coffee and then he invited back to his hotel.

"I am sorry, Erik but it's getting late and I am sure my friends must be worried about me." He looked quite disappointed but I think he sort of understood.

I called Luis Fernando and he soon came to pick me up. I gave Erik a big hug and we said goodbye. We didn't even exchange numbers as we knew we would probably never meet again.

"Who was that?" asked Luis Fernando.

"A Canadian I met and we just spent all the afternoon together; it has been a lot of fun." Luis Fernando gave me "the look" but Anita just smiled and said: "He was very handsome; you should have invited him home to have dinner with us."

"Too late now and I don't even know his mobile number."

"What a shame."

I was a bit disappointed as I would have loved to see more of Erik.

The following morning, we took a long time to get ready as we had to pack sleeping bags and tents and food and lots of clothes as Luis Fernando said it would be very cold in the evening. The road to Wiñaymarka was similar to the one going to Tiwanaku but we took a turn close to the Lake and we started following its shore line.

During our journey Luis Fernando told me how he had an encounter with ETs and he was told of the existence of a retreat run by the Elders here at Lake Titicaca, The Elders were from the pre-Incan 'Tiwanaku civilization', and were also the final remnants of the even older Atlantean civilization. He also said how he was asked to build the retreat here by the lake and how by a series of "coincidences" he was able to purchase the land near Huarina, located in the minor part of the lake and build Wiñaymarka.

We arrived at Wiñaymarka in the middle of the afternoon, set in the shores of the lake and with beautiful views of it; there was the construction of a temple with a huge monolithic structure in the middle. After setting up the tents and having something to eat, Anita and Luis Fernando did a series of rituals and guided meditations and I was able to feel the remarkable energies of this spectacular and remote place. During the evening we stayed by the fire sky-gazing, it was very cold and I thought it was going to be very difficult for me to sleep there. Then we saw a number of UFOs and one in particular flared up a beam of light right to where we were and almost immediately I felt a soothing warm energy surrounding me, as if they had read my mind, and I was able to have a very relaxing and sound deep sleep.

The following morning, after a meditation and breakfast, we took a boat trip to an inhabited island which according to Luis Fernando is the closest physical point to both the Lake Titicaca Lodge of the Great White Brotherhood and a Galactic Confederation Base. At the Island, we did a number of exercises, which allowed us to energetically connect with the ascended masters at the Great White Brotherhood Lodge. He also explained to me that at the Lodge the brotherhood kept several important artefacts from Earth's history.

We then returned to La Paz. I was feeling like a new person, full of energy and I felt more relaxed than I have ever felt before in my life.

During our dinner Luis Fernando said that I should delay my flight to Lima as there were more places that I should see in Bolivia.

"You must visit the Island of the Sun and the Island of the Moon in Lake Titicaca and the Sajama Volcano, the Thermal waters of Urmi, such special sites but the most amazing place here in Bolivia is El Salar de Uyuni> It's the highest concentration of salt on Earth and where the earth meets the sky, there is a time during the rainy season when you cannot differentiate between the sky and the earth. The Astronaut Neil Armstrong saw it from space as the shiniest place on earth and he even travelled there as he had to go and see it for himself."

"Maybe next time, as I have all my flights booked already."

"You are always welcome to come and visit, or maybe you can join one of my retreats of Solar Activation, I hold them every six months and really nice people always come to those events, or join me on any of my journeys around the world. I publish them on my webpage and on social media, but we will always be in touch, it's been amazing meeting you and I am sure we will meet again, and thank you again for all your help in the UK."

The following morning, Luis Fernando and Anita drove for the very last time to El Alto, towards the airport. There was more traffic than usual and I thought I would miss my flight. My heart was beating fast and Luis Fernando was trying to drive as fast as he could, dodging all the traffic and when we finally reached the airport, we hugged and both Anita and I shed some tears. It had been so nice meeting her, and spending such a wonderful time with them in this magical place called Bolivia. I knew it wasn't really a goodbye but a see you later.

Queueing up at the airport to catch my flight, I thought I recognized someone,

"Hello, Gorgeous."

"Erik! What on earth are you doing here?"

"Same as you, travelling to Peru."

Peru, Lima

Erik queued with me while I checked-in as he had already done so, we cleared emigration and then we sat in a cafeteria waiting for the boarding of our flight to be announced. He was looking rather charming; he had cleaned up from the time we met in La Paz. I could see his hair was lighter - a bit like the cappuccino I was drinking and his eyes matched the colour of his hair.

"So, Gaby, tell me what you do in London?"

"I run a yoga centre with a friend of mine, who is looking after the place as we speak."

"No wonder you have such an amazing figure, I bet you have a very healthy lifestyle."

"I do try, but it's not always easy, especially whilst travelling, so many temptations along the way and I've heard the Peruvian cuisine is particularly good, it has become very popular in London.

"Well, we better find a good restaurant in Lima, although I like street food, I find it tastier, even though is not always the healthiest."

"I'm not sure my stomach agrees with street food."

"Oh, well you can stay with me in Lima and I will find out a good restaurant that agrees with your delicate digestive system", Erik said rather sarcastically:

And what do you do in Toronto?" I asked Erik, as I needed to change the subject. I wasn't quite sure I wanted to spend all my time in Lima with him, although he was so nice, there was something about him that was very attractive, I could feel some connection with him but, I didn't want to end just in bed and goodbye see you never again, as usual.

"I work in air cons," Erik said without any enthusiasm, he was probably a plumber and now a backpacker but at least he was nice.

Our flight was announced and there was a very long queue.

"Better wait, we have seats reserved so what is the point in rushing," Erik said glued to his seat.

"Knowing me I would have been there right at the front of the queue," I said laughing. Finally, when there were just a few people left to board, Erik stood up.

As we were going into the plane, he looked at my ticket.

"Where are you seated?"

"22A, I like a window seat, and you?" he didn't reply, but then he turned left, and I stood there gobsmacked; never judge a book by its cover.

I walked down the aisle until I reached my seat, the plane was very full and I had to ask the two people in my row to stand up and let me in. I was particularly embarrassed as the lady sitting right next to me was holding a baby.

I sat down and just stared out the window, thinking how we never should judge people by their appearance, how we judge other races and cultures, who knows, who is right, deep down we are all the same, we come from the same source and maybe in another lifetime we could have belong to the same race and culture of the one that we are harshly judging.

The plane took off and once again I was admiring the majestic mountains of the Andean chain ridge, once the seat belt sign went off, I saw Erik strolling down the aisle searching for me, when he finally saw me, he started talking to the lady with the baby sitting right next to me.

"Would you mind swapping your seat with me? I have just over two hours to persuade this beautiful lady sitting next to you, to spend the next few days with me in Lima." She looked a bit startled, as she didn't know what to do, and the baby was starting to cry, probably not happy about all the commotion.

"Come on, let me help you out," said Erik as he bent down to hold the baby. "I am in first class and I can assure you will be more comfortable there and I will ask the flight attendants to take good care of you and your baby." When she heard the word "first class" she immediately stood up, handed the baby to Erik and grabbed her things. Erik went with her and he came back five minutes later.

He had a big grin in his face; he sat next to me and held my hand.

"Well, now Gaby why don't you spend the next few days with me in Lima? You can stay in my hotel, I'm booked in the Lima Marriot Hotel in Miraflores, it's a 5-star hotel overlooking the Pacific Ocean?"

"Look Erik, the fact that you are not a plumber and a mere backpacker doesn't make me change my mind. I already have a reservation in a humble accommodation, it's called Pension Miraflores, so I am probably not too far from you, and as it's already paid for and I can't afford your 5-star luxury hotel I will keep to my reservation, thank you."

"God, you are stubborn. At least the lady sitting here was only too happy to be upgraded to first class."

"I didn't ask you to give up your seat; I hope you are not regretting it now."

"I'm going to strangle you in a minute, Women, who ever created you, must have had a really good laugh doing so."

"The fact that I am not upgrading to a 5-star hotel doesn't mean we can't go out while in Lima. I just don't want to hop into your bed straight away, maybe you are used to it, and maybe I would have done so before but I promised to myself I wouldn't do it anymore."

"Fair enough Lady Gaby, so what do you fancy doing, besides finding a good restaurant, although I did book a table for 2 tomorrow just in case in the famous Central restaurant, it's ranked amongst the 10 best restaurants in the world, so I made sure that I could get a table a few weeks ago."

"I'm only staying 3 days in Lima before flying to Cuzco, and I didn't really check out what to do in Lima. I just thought I could walk around the city and go to a few museums. In Cuzco a friend of mine did put me in contact with a Shaman and he is supposed to show me around all the Inca sites. I'll stay there five days, then down the Valley of the Incas, a short five day Inca Trail hike all the way to Machu Pichu and then I'll stay in the adjoining town, Aguas Calientes for a couple of days and then back to Cuzco and back home. So, you see there is not much room for romance in this trip. I didn't plan to bump into you in the Cathedral in La Paz, and never thought our paths would cross again, and then, you live in Toronto and I live in London." I said rather disenchanted with it all.

"Where is your sense of adventure, and taking risks in life and just going for it, I really thought you were that kind of girl, travelling all by yourself around South America." Erik sounded a bit disappointed, and probably regretting having moved next to me. I looked out of the window and wondered the same thing, where had the happy go lucky Gaby gone, I had to find her inside me somehow. We didn't talk much after that, when we landed in Lima, Erik just said:

"At least let me drive you to your hotel," we got in the taxi and he held my hand. I thought he was very sweet, what was wrong with me, there was a really nice guy sitting next to me and I had become this lump of ice. When the taxi stopped in front of Pension Miraflores, we both looked at each other, it was a complete dump shack.

"It's not exactly how it looked in the internet when I booked it." I was in shock.

"Gaby, I will not let leave you in this place no matter what, even if you don't want to share the bed and I have to sleep in the couch, you are coming with me;" he asked the taxi driver to move on and I was relieved that I wasn't staying there but I had butterflies in my stomach. We arrived at the Marriot hotel, and Erik explained at the counter that I was staying in his room, but that he would like an extra bed if possible. The concierge gave me a funny look and asked for my passport, he opened it and just kept staring at me, he finally handed me back my passport and I was given a copy of the keys. Our room had the most fantastic views of the Pacific Ocean and all you could hear was the sound of crashing waves on the pebbled beach, it was very modern and sleek with a huge king size bed in the middle of the room. Erik opened his bag and took a few clothes out:

"I'm going to take a shower and then I will go downstairs to try and sort out a good restaurant for us to eat, and give you some space for you to freshen up. I will meet you at reception later." After taking a shower he left the room without saying anything else.

I took my mobile out and sure enough I had quite a few emails and messages, looked straight at Linda's name and there were none from her. "Are you all right Linda?" I asked her.

"Yes, just thought I will give you a break about my saga. I'm enjoying just watching my belly grow; the Italians have a good phrase for that: "Dolce far niente" The sweetness of doing nothing! You must be in Lima now?"

"I'm in Lima staying in the JW Marriot with the most amazing guy I met in La Paz and that happened to be in the same flight and I have been horrible to him and now, I don't know how to straighten things up."

"Don't tell me you have lost your magic touch, so unlike you, go and dress up to kill; I hope you packed your red matador outfit."

"No, I didn't think I would meet anyone, not on this trip, I'll have a look to see what I can find?"

"That's my girl, darling, go after him and put on your best charming smile to go with the outfit."

"Love you."

"Keep me updated."

I turned off my mobile and went straight to my bag and found a nice blue dress and although I hadn't packed any and high heel shoes, I had a pair of pretty sandals. I looked in the mirror:

"Gaby, go for it! He is a good guy, don't waist anymore time," I winked at myself and left the room.

Erik was talking to the concierge and they both looked at me from top to bottom.

"You are looking gorgeous," Erik said and I could feel myself blushing. "I was talking to Carlos and he recommended a few places for us to eat, we could go to Chinatown as the Chinese restaurants here are quite famous, they are called Chifas and they are a fusion between Japanese, Chinese and Peruvian cuisines or, we could go to Huaca Pucllana, a traditional Peruvian restaurant set-in front of Inca ruins, or to Vista al Mar, that has stunning views of the Pacific Ocean, also Peruvian food, you choose please Gaby as I can't make up my mind."

"They all sound amazing, but the one in front of the ruins is the one that sound like an exciting experience."

We walked out of the hotel to take a taxi and in amongst the queue of taxis there was a tuck-tuck, I walked straight to it and jumped inside it.

"I love a tuck-tuck. I think is the best way to travel in a city." Erik gave me a big smile and sat next to me, and as the driver pulled out quite abruptly, I held on tight to Erik, he looked at me and said with a big grin on his face:

"And they have just become my favourite too."

The driver smiled and said in perfect English, "I can pick you up later from the restaurant and I can give you a good tour around Lima."

"Maybe tomorrow," said Erik, as the restaurant is not far from the hotel, I think I would just like to walk back to it, let's say 9am, is that okay with you?"

"I'll be waiting for you, I will take you to see all of Lima, and you won't regret it."

The ride to the restaurant was just a few minutes, but Erik gave the driver a big tip which made him very happy.

"Do you always give big tips?" I asked him.

"Only in third world countries as I know they probably have big families to support and I am sure they could do with the extra money."

"A friend once told me not to haggle in the markets either as that is also their only income and I have never haggled again unless I am clearly being ripped off."

We walked inside the restaurant and were taken to a table right in front of the ruins; it felt quite bizarre sitting there amongst ancient ruins.

"Don't they all look quite alike, Tiwanaku, Egypt, Tikal, Stonehenge, Machu Pichu, all made out of stone and set with amazing precision all those thousands of years ago, I do wonder how they all came about with such similarities, dotted all around the world?" said Erik just gazing at them.

"According to my friend Luis Fernando, extra-terrestrials have a lot to do with it," I said very casually.

"Could be, as the architects seem to have met each other at one point, or could have been star seeds," said Erik.

"What are star seeds?"

"Have you ever felt like Earth is not your home, and you always have that longing inside that you want to go home, but you can't really pinpoint where home is, maybe another planet, you always feel out of place and nobody really understands you and you love being alone, in peace and with nature and avoid crowded places, you have always been fascinated by space and science-fiction movies?"

"That is me. I love Star Wars and Star Trek, anything like that and I would be the first one to go and watch it."

"So, you prefer to watch the sky, rather than being anywhere else? Star seeds are souls of extra-terrestrial origin that have come to assist earth, by spreading their knowledge. I believe all the amazing technological advances that we have now, such as the internet, didn't originate here on planet earth but elsewhere from the Universe and Steve Job, Albert Einstein, Bill Gates, Tim Berners-Lee and many more could have been star seeds."

"Wow, you are full of surprises, how come you know about all of these things, never though you would be interested in extra-terrestrials." I looked at Erik and just wondered who he really was, and bumping into him in a church in La Paz and then having to be on the same flight, seemed to me that there was more to this encounter than just a mere coincidence. I think I better keep my eyes wide open.

Our food arrived and throughout dinner I told Erik all about Luis Fernando and Glastonbury, the Crop Circles, Wiñaymarka and all the spaceship sightings.

"I wished I had met him, and to think that I was so close, I have dreamt all my life of seeing a spaceship, I have always gazed at the stars and wondered who else is out there and I've always had this longing as if somewhere out there is my real home. I started searching on the internet and that is how I came across star seeds, as the one thing all star seeds have in common is that we are always feeling out of place on this planet, as if we don't belong here, that is why I believe I might be a star seed and now I meet you, my beautiful fellow star seed."

"I have only just started to find out about extra-terrestrials myself but I've always had this feeling that there is more to life that what is right in front of me and I've always longed for more and more." I said to

Erik just realizing that I always felt that there was something missing in my life.

We walked holding hands along the seafront towards our hotel, and we sat on the embankment just staring at the sky, when suddenly a bolt of light that seemed to come out of nowhere sparked in the sky.

"Wow, what was that?" asked a very surprised Erik.

"They are just letting us know that they are there, and they are watching over us."

I turned round and looked at Erik and he just held my face and gave me a very sweet long kiss and I felt a bolt of light had just hit me and I realized I had met the love of my life, he looked at me and there were tears in his eyes, as if he had just realized the same thing too. We stayed there hugging for a long time, there was no rush to go back to the hotel, we just wanted to embrace there as one for all eternity. When we eventually got back to our hotel, we saw that someone had set a small bed in the corner of our bedroom; we looked at it and laughed. We slowly took our clothes off and we kept looking at each other caressing all of our bodies, it was not just making love, it was the union of two souls that had been searching for each other and had finally met. The following morning, we woke up and we were just staring at each other, when the phone rang. It was the concierge letting us know that the tuck-tuck driver had arrived and was waiting for us.

"I wished we had not booked the tuck-tuck driver, I just want to stay here in bed with you all day", said Erik holding me tight.

"Come on, we have all of our lives to be together, but just this one chance to go and see Lima."

"I hope you really mean what you just said."

"The bit that we only have this chance to go and see Lima?" I winked at him and jumped into the shower.

As we were going out of the hotel Erik handed the keys to Carlos the concierge, "No need for the extra bed in our room, you can ask the housekeeper to re-move it, thanks."

"Will do and have a good day," he looked at me, but this time he gave me a smile.

The tuck-tuck driver was waiting for us with a ra-diant smile, I am not sure what is it with tuck-tuck drivers but they all seem to have a contagious smile.

"Bueno días, I hope you are looking forward to the best tour of Lima, one of the largest cities in La-tin America, that has just about everything you can think of, as you can see it has this amazing setting in front of the Pacific Ocean, and your hotel offers the best views of the cliffs and the sea, so I am going to take you straight to the Plaza Mayor of Lima located in the Historic Centre of Lima, surrounded by the Go-vernment Palace, Cathedral of Lima, Archbishop's Pa-lace of Lima, the Municipal Palace, and the Palace of the Union Afterwards I can take you to the Larco Mu-seum that holds a large collection of Pre-Columbian artefacts and maybe then I can show you around old Lima, the places that not many tourist go to see. What do you think?"

"I think we can skip the museum as we are going to Cusco and Machu Pichu and I am sure we will see lots of artefacts there. I would rather see the old town; you can take us to all those secret places that are less popular with tourists." Erik looked at me for my approval. I just nodded and smiled; I like a man that takes charge but is also thoughtful. We set about admiring this amazing city that has such a mixture of the old and the new, the traffic was chaotic but our driver just dodged all the traffic jams whilst I held very tight to Erik. In the old town we went to visit The House of St. Martin de Porres and the driver explained that Saint Martin was the illegitimate son of a Spanish nobleman, Don Juan de Porres y de la Peña and Ana Velázquez, and was treated very badly as he was of mixed race and illegitimate. He was not allowed to go to a mainstream school and the church never allowed him to take Holy Orders to become a full priest. He dedicated his life to the care of the poor of Lima and many miracles were attributed to him, especially when an epidemic struck Lima and there were 60 friars who were sick in the Convent of the Rosary, who were locked in a section of the convent. St. Martin is said to have passed through the locked doors to care for them. He also founded a residence for orphans and abandoned children in the city of Lima. After he died, there were so many miracles attributed to him that his body was exhumed after twenty five years and was supposedly found intact, and exuding a fine fragrance. Letters to Rome pleaded for his beatification and he was finally beatified by Pope Gregory XVI and Pope John XXIII canonized him in Rome on the sixth of May 1962. The museum and the church were amazing but then the driver took us through very small alleys and he showed us a huge mural of St. Martin where he had supposedly appeared.

"If you stand here and prey to him, he will make your dreams come true," said the driver. "I often come here and he has granted me many miracles," he said almost crying.

Erik held my hand and kissed it. "My miracle has already been granted to me as I met this beautiful woman in a cathedral, clearly a match made in heaven and now ratified here in front of this wonderful mural of one of the most remarkable saints in history."

I choked as I heard Erik say those words, and I closed my eyes and asked St. Martin to help me work things out in my life but most of all to help Linda in the difficult time in her life with her pregnancy and that as her child would be born an illegitimate child, he could make Tom come to his senses and recognise his child.

As we were walking back to the tuck-tuck we passed a jewellery shop and Erik went straight in, and for a moment I thought he might buy a ring and propose there and then, but then he asked the shopkeeper to show him some golden stars.

"Choose one; it's for you to remember that you are a star seed."

"In that case I will buy one for you, so you can remember the same too."

We both went out of the shop wearing our beautiful star seed pendants. I felt so proud as if I had received a golden star back at school for good behaviour.

"What do you think?" I asked the driver, "and can you please tell me your name?"

"Better put them away as there are many pickpockets around her and my name is Luis Alfonso but my friends call me Lucho".

I put my golden star inside my t-shirt and Erik did the same, better be safe than sorry.

"Lucho, can you recommend a place for us to have lunch? I'm starving."

"We are not far from Chinatown or the street food around here is very good."

I looked at all the places on the street and saw lots of flies and dust around them.

"I think Chinatown will be good, the concierge at the hotel recommended it last night." Erik said as if he was reading my mind.

We walked through the narrow streets of Chinatown and we ate in one of the restaurants along the main street, we ordered lots of food and when the plates were served, they were huge - not like the small portions served in the restaurants in London; we all looked at each other and laughed. We ate what we could, it was delicious, and Lucho asked if he could take home all the left-overs.

"My wife loves Chinese food it will be a really good treat for her and the children," he said with a big green on his face.

"In that case let me order some more for you to take home," Erik said while he called the waiter and ordered lots more food for Lucho to take to his family.

We had difficulty finding a place for all the food in the tuck-tuck, but just to see Lucho's happy face made it all worthwhile.

We asked Lucho to take us back to our hotel; he gave us a big hug when we said our goodbyes as we wouldn't need him anymore.

"We are going to Cusco tomorrow and I'm afraid that all our luggage won't fit in the tuck-tuck." Erik paid him and gave him double what he asked for and I could see that Lucho was a bit tearful.

As we went in to the hotel, Erik asked me for my travel documents.

"I want to change my flights to your itinerary and also upgrade you as I don't really want to squeeze in those small seats at the back."

"Snob, there is nothing wrong with the seats at the back of a plane," I winked at him.

"It's my legs; they are too long for those tight seats at the back."

I handed him my flight tickets: "I am not going to say no to the upgrade this time; I've always wondered what it was like to turn left in an airplane."

Erik took his phone and lap-top and after a while he closed it. "All done, I've booked you all the way back to London in business class." He handed me back my tickets: "I've also booked nice hotels in Cusco and Aguas Calientes; yours looked just as bad as Pension Miraflores." He was staring at me. "Now, we have a problem, remember I said I had reservations for this evening at the famous Central restaurant, one of the best restaurants in the world but, I am very full and I much rather stay here with you."

"Well, better cancel the reservation in the most famous restaurant in the world, I much rather stay here with you too."

Cusco

Pedro, the Shaman that Lucia had recommended, was waiting for us at the airport. After I introduced him to Erik, he gave him a good look all around him, making a few gestures.

"He is acceptable, and good job I speak good English; I spent some time in California, but had to come back to my beautiful Andes and simpler way of living."

I just laughed and told him where to go.

"But I thought you were staying at Pension Don Bosco?"

"Erik changed the reservations". He gave Erik the look, as he had made the original reservation.

"I think the JW Marriott El Convento Cusco is the best hotel in Cusco and it was highly recommended by a friend," said Erik.

"Yes, it's a very good hotel but I don't think they will like me hanging around there very much, I know everyone in the Pension and I feel more comfortable there."

"I haven't cancelled the reservation in the Pension, we can go there during the day and you can sleep there if you want to as it's all paid for but we can sleep in the hotel as it's also been booked and paid for."

"That sounds great, then I don't have to go back to my farmhouse every day as it's a long way away."

"You see Pedro, it is all for the best!" I said giving him a big smile.

We jumped into a very old jeep that looked as if it was falling apart and sounded even worse once we started moving. Pedro just gave us a reassuring look.

"Don't worry, this beauty has never let me down and it's well blessed by me."

We started going through the street of Cusco, a beautifully preserved colonial city.

"Cusco was the capital of the Inca Empire until the Spanish arrived in the 16th century and destroyed all the Inca temples by building on top of them, but there are still remnants of the great walls of the Incas, there was a major earthquake that hit Cusco on the 21st of May 1950, that caused damage to most of the city's structures. The Dominican Priory and Church of Santo Domingo, which were built on top of the impressive *Qurikancha,* the Temple of the Sun, were amongst the affected colonial era buildings but, the Inca architecture withstood the earthquake." Pedro said with great pride.

We arrived at the hotel, an impressive colonial building as I walked in, I was left speechless, the tasteful restoration of the convent was astounding. Pedro was somewhat shy as he walked in with us.

"I will wait by the jeep outside Mr Erik," he said very politely.

Erik held Pedro by his arm and as he checked he told the concierge that Pedro was our guide and friend and would be accompanying us throughout our stay. The concierge gave a nod and a smile to Pedro that seemed to feel better after that.

"Pedro, we are going up to quickly drop our things and will be back in 20 minutes. In the meantime you can have a drink or anything you want, although we would like to have something to eat soon. Is it better here or shall we go somewhere else?"

Pedro took a good look at the beautiful courtyard, "We can have something here, and I can always start ordering some starters for when you come down again."

"Great, see you soon," Erik winked at him.

I went into the bedroom and was gobsmacked; it was probably the best hotel I had stayed in my life. "Wow, this is amazing Erik, I don't want to even asked how much it costs."

"Just enjoy it, and hurry up we don't want to leave Pedro waiting too long."

We arrived back at the courtyard and Pedro had ordered every starter on the menu. "I'm a vegetarian so you and Erik can eat the meat ones and I will try all the veggie ones."

"No problem with that, I can eat anything," said Pedro as he started gobbling up a bit of everything.

"Today I thought I could take you around Cusco. We can just walk around as everything is quite close, the Plaza de Armas, the Cathedral, churches, the barrio de San Blas, and some of the Inca walls built with amazing precision by them. Many of the colonial structures used the city's Inca constructions as a base. I will do all the tourist things today, but tomorrow, I will take you to the Valley of the Moon where we can perform a ceremony as it's not a place where tourist goes and it's a sacred place for us the descendants of the great Incas, but the day after tomorrow I am sure the reason why you came here is to attend the Inti Raymi."

"The Inti Raymi, what on earth is that?" I asked Pedro as Erik and I both looked at each other with a startled face.

"You are telling me that you are here now in Cusco and you haven't got any idea of what the Inti Raymi is?" asked Pedro very surprised and rubbing his head. "The Inti *Raymi is a religious ceremony in honour of the God Inti, the most venerated deity of* the Incas, in celebration of the winter solstice. In Quechua *Inti* means Sun and *Raymi* celebration. Inti Raymi is the celebration of the God Sun. Pachatutec, the first Inca, created the Inti Raymi to celebrate the first day of the New Year in the Inca calendar. The festival takes place on the Fortress of Sacsayhuaman, and you better ask the concierge now if they still have any tickets available." Pedro kept shaking his head in disbelief.

Erik stood up and ran to the concierge and a while later he came back with a big grin in his face and holding two tickets.

"Pedro, I forgot to ask you, do you need a ticket too?"

Pedro just gave Erik "the look". "I am walking with my tribe, no need for me to get a ticket."

"Right, we better start walking around Cusco. I'm dying to see it all," I said just to calm Pedro down.

We started walking around the beautiful colonial city with its mixture of Spanish and Inca legacies. We found some walls on the narrow alley of Loreto, with Inca walls on each side, but the most impressive walls were located on Hatunrumiyoc Street, named after the popular "Twelve Angled Stone." It was amazing to think how these were precisely cut, shaped and assembled to fit so perfectly well that even a sheet of paper wouldn't fit between them. It made me think again at the resemblance of the Ancient Pyramids of Giza, Stonehenge, and Tiwanaku and thought again of the influence they might have had from the stars.

"These large stones were once part of an Inca palace; can you imagine how beautiful the palace must have looked like? It always saddens me to think about it. There are so many places that have been destroyed by man but the worst miscarriage of justice is what we are all doing to Pachamama. Tomorrow we will send her love and healing, I am really looking forward to sharing the energy of this place with you," said Pedro, letting us know that there was more to this place that what you can see here in Cusco.

We arrived at the Plaza de Armas, a lovely square with well-maintained gardens and a statue of Pachacuti, the Inca ruler. The square is surrounded by restaurants, bars, coffee shops and even a large Starbucks. There are 3 churches including the impressive Cathedral, we went inside it and it didn't disappoint, it's one of the most beautiful I have ever seen, especially the high altar and a magnificent fresco of the last supper. We then took a short walk from the plaza to Cusco's San Pedro Market, one of the city's most popular attractions. The indoor market had several sections with many food stalls and vendors. I was in my element and wanted to buy everything.

"I will leave you two here as I know you would like to spend some time looking around and I am not interested in anything here. Be careful, they will offer you all sorts of magic treatments and experiences, and take it from me; they are all scammers trying to earn some quick dollars from the tourists. There are a few food vendors but it is better if you go back to the Plaza de Armas and eat in one of the restaurants there, the food here might come with a bacterium or two and I don't want you to get a tummy upset. I will pick you up tomorrow at your hotel around 9 am, wear hiking boots and a good coat, also ask the hotel to prepare a picnic basket, and a flask of coca tea." Pedro gave us hug and left.

By the time we arrived at the hotel, we were so tired that we fell asleep straight away and it wasn't until we received the call from the concierge letting us know that Pedro was waiting that we woke up. We all had breakfast together and Pedro gave the instructions to the waiter as what to pack for our lunch; he was feeling quite at home now in this grand hotel.

I was quite anxious as I had not had time to look at my mobile and was worried about Linda. As soon as I turned the phone on and connected to the internet it started bleeping none stopped. Most of the messages were from Linda.

"Where are you?" "Are you OK?" "Have you been kidnapped by the Canadian?"

"Hi, Linda, I have been kidnapped by the Canadian but in the most delightful way, I think I am in love this time, truly in love. I will tell you all about it when I have the chance to write. How are you, the baby, Tom, are you still at my flat, let me know? Love you, Gaby".

There were also a few messages from George.

"At least say Hi!"

"Hi George, I am in Cusco now with Pedro, I am sure all is well at the centre, kisses Gaby."

I turned it off and put in my bag.

"Anything interesting?" asked Erik trying to find out who I was chatting to.

"A few boyfriends… just teasing, my friend Linda and my partner George. And you, I haven't seen you trying to contact anyone, not even your Mum?"

"I don't want to spoil my time here with you, I can only guess all the problems back home, it's best not to know."

"Erik is right, it's best to enjoy the moment and not bring your vibration down with things that you can't do anything about right now; better go and raise those vibrations even more." Pedro stood up picking up the lovely picnic basket the hotel had prepared for us.

We all jumped into the jeep and drove off up the hill and from the top of the mountains I could see how big Cusco actually was, set amongst very lush green mountains, and thought how the Conquistadors managed to find it so high up in the wild Andean Mountain Range on horseback. We drove past a few hamlets and dotted around you could see Inca ruins. I asked Pedro about them.

"The Inca Empire called Tawantinsuyu in Quechua was the largest Empire in the Americas, the administrative centre was Cusco, and it extended from northern Chile to the tip of Colombia and went as far as Argentina, it was all connected by an extensive road network. They were extremely successful and worked together with Pachamama and knew all about crops and how to grow good and healthy foods, they had no money but worked solely on trade exchanging with each other what they needed, there was no greed, there was a lot of knowledge about healing plants and the use of energy to cure the sick, and I truly believe that one day we will return to this way of living, it's the only way that earth will flourish once again."

"The Incas were so advanced, I also hope that one day we will return to their way of life, it seemed that they knew much more than we do right now. How did they know all about construction and healing, they didn't have cranes, or tractors or mortar, nor did they have books, where on earth did, they learnt all these things?" I asked Pedro.

"Gaby, they looked to the stars for help and also going within, two things that most of us have forgotten to do."

I told Pedro all about Luis Fernando and my experiences in Bolivia.

"Tiwanaku was a civilization earlier than the Incas that were also guided by our friends from the stars. I can often see them around here, maybe we could try and contact them tonight, and we can go to my farm when we finish here in the Valley of the Moon, but I don't want to stay up too late as I have a busy day tomorrow with the Inti Raymi."

"That would be fantastic and a dream come true for me, I have always wanted to see them, I believe we are star seeds and would love to contact my friends from above too," said an overjoyed Erik.

We arrived at an esplanade with a few rocks around and a mountain that looked a bit like South Africa's Table Mountain in miniature placed on top of the Andes, the sun was shining right on top of it and it looked as it was made of pure gold. There was a lake in front of it and the reflection in the water made the whole place so bright that it was difficult to see. We started walking towards it, we climbed and went all around it to the other side until we found an entrance to a cave, before we went in Pedro asked permission to go in and took a small bag from his rucksack, he took some feathers out and did a short dance, clearing out the space before he invited us inside the small cave. He drew a circle on the ground with a sharp knife and invited me and Erik to sit inside the circle.

"I asked permission to the Apu, the spirit of this temple to bless Erik and Gaby," he said as he took a small clay jar and placed some crystals and coca leaves inside it, he also cut a bit of his hair, of mine and Erik's and placed them inside the jar together with some incense, he lit the contents of the jar and started singing and blessing us, the energy of the place was immense and I could feel tears down my cheeks, I looked at Erik and I could see that he was also crying. When the leaves were almost burnt, he took them out of the jar and placed them on the ground.

"The Apu has spoken through the leaves, he foresees a great future for both of you, this is a union of two souls bound together for eternity, and you will together bring awareness to a great many, rest assured that this is not a coincidence, you had planned this before you incarnated and it is now time for you to fulfil your mission here on Earth." He took two crystals that were inside the jar and gave one each to me and Erik; he then made a small hole in the centre of the circle and buried the jar together with the leaves. He stood up thanked the Apu and gave us both a big hug.

"That was really a beautiful message, thank you, Pedro," I said to him, I was holding Erik's hand but he couldn't stop crying and just walked out of the cave and went down and sat next to the lake.

Pedro and I walked back to the jeep and waited a few minutes until he came back.

"Sorry about that, the energy was too intense."

"No need to apologize, brother, you have a beautiful soul. We are going to my farm now, it's not far from here, and I am very hungry and can't wait to try everything inside the picnic basket."

We drove back towards Cusco and took a short diversion through a dirt road until we found a small shack, there were a few hens that came running towards Pedro as soon as he stepped down from the jeep.

"My baby girls, you must all be so hungry," he took a bag of maize and gave them some; he was talking to them as if they were his best friends.

"That is another sign that you are a star seed, you have a great compassion for all animals, I think that you Pedro, are also a star seed," said Erik holding his star.

The shack was very basic but clean, I asked for a toilet and he said that there was small hut outside, I went out and at the bottom of a garden there was a "toilet" made out of hay, but it was clean. The garden had rows and rows of crops set within raised beds made of stone. There were tomatoes, green beans, corn, chilies, lots and lots of potato plants, and all sorts of herbs and things I had no idea what they were. Pedro came out and lit a fire, we sat on a wooden table and he placed a very colourful hand-woven table cloth and the basket on top. The hotel had packed just about everything, including plates and cutlery. Pedro opened the flask of coca tea that was still hot, and poured some on each cup. He raised his cup and dropped some on the ground.

"This is for the Apu, may you bless the food we are about to eat..."

"Amen."

We all ate and talked about our lives. I told Pedro about my yoga centre and Erik about his job and his mother.

When night came, Pedro started to chant and dance around the fire and soon enough we started noticing a few lights moving in the sky, one of them sent a bolt of light towards us.

"They say that you should look out for them as they will be showing up for you in the Isles of Avalon."

Erik and I started cheering and waving towards them.

And then they left… and so did we. We went back to Cusco and our hotel.

Morning arrived with the sounds of drums and music coming from the street. We looked out of the window and we could see that the parade had started. We rushed downstairs and the concierge explained that the festival started at 8am in the Plaza de Armas but then there would be a procession, where the Sapa Inca would be carried on a throne followed by all the tribes to the Fortress of Sacsayhuaman, there they would perform many rituals to thank the Sun for his generosity. He said the bus that would take us to the fortress would leave in one hour and that we had plenty of time to have breakfast.

We arrived at the fortress and we had a fantastic view of the whole event, it was so colourful and having the fortress as a backdrop was breath-taking. We could see Pedro at a distance with one of the tribes; he looked amazing wearing his full Indian costume. The Sapa Inca talks to each tribal chief holding them accountable for their actions during the year and each tribe performs a dance for the Sapa Inca. It was a lovely way to spend the last day before setting off on the Inca Trail.

Machu Picchu

The tour operator brought a small bag to the hotel for us to pack our things for the Inca Trail.

"You can only pack five kilos maximum, and also a swimming costume, in case you want to have dip in one of the rivers, there are no showers or toilets during the 4-day trek, you can leave the rest of your things here at the hotel, and a van will take all your luggage latter on to your hotel in Aguas Calientes. I will pick you up tomorrow at 8 am."

At 8 am, Juan, our tour guide, picked us from the hotel.

"Today we are going to the Sacred Valley, we will stop along the way in a few places and we will spend the night in a hotel in the settlement of Ollantaytambo, there we will be joined there by other people."

"That sound great," I said, whilst Erik was still half asleep in the 4x4.

It took a while to leave Cusco due to heavy traffic but soon after the magnificent view of the Andean mountains was there like a painting for us to admire. Our first stop was Chincheros where we saw terracing for vegetable-growing down into the valley with rugged mountains beyond; it just amazed me how they managed to grow crops in the most difficult terrains;

the crops consistent mainly of different types of potatoes and corn. The village itself was really charming. The main square was full of sellers and woven goods made mainly from alpaca wool. All the women were dressed in their traditional costumes and were only too happy to have their pictures taken for a few dollars.

There was a bit of a drive then to our lunchtime stop, Urubamba - a beautiful place with well-tended gardens and an excellent buffet with plenty of veggie options. We sat next to another couple, it was great talking to them and we learnt that they were also walking the Inca Trail with us the following morning.

"I'm Richard and this is my wife Clara, we live in Manchester in the UK but my wife is Colombian."

"Nice to meet you. I am Erik. I am from Toronto and this is my girlfriend Gaby, she comes from London." Erik said smiling at me, it was the first time he had introduced me as his girlfriend and I couldn't stop giggling.

We all started talking about our lives and laughing a bit, when Clara asked:

"What are those stars you are wearing?"

"We are star seeds," said Erik as a matter of fact.

"So are we," they said in unison, as they both showed us their matching star pendants beautifully enamelled with bright colours on silver.

"Talk about coincidences, let us hope this is the beginning of a long and lasting friendship," I said raising my glass of water.

"Cheers!"

Juan came by and said: "Sorry guys but we have to keep going, there is still a long way to go before we reach our destination."

We all hugged, and just said: "See you tomorrow."

After lunch we drove along the Urubamba River valley, until we arrived at the settlement of Ollantaytambo. The Incas had built steps up to a sun gate at the top, it was hard a climbing up the uneven steps but well worth the spectacular views from the top; so many mountains, one had a face cut into the rock and dwellings perched up the mountainside that looked as if they were about to slide off. We climbed down and Juan drove us to our retreat for the night, a lovely wooden ranch set at the far end of the village.

"You better have a good night sleep, it's going to be four hard days walking through very difficult terrain before you reach Machu Picchu; your guide will come and pick you up at 6 am tomorrow morning, it's been a pleasure meeting you."

We said our goodbyes and Erik and I me went straight to our room, we ordered a light snack, had a lovely warm relaxing bath and fell asleep.

A knock at our door at 5:30 am woke us up.

"Better get ready and have something to eat before you go", a sweet lady's voice whispered from the other side of the door.

We came out and there was a strong smell of chocolate coming from the kitchen, the ranch was very rustic but very clean. The lady, all dressed up in her colourful traditional dress, brought us the chocolate and some lovely buns and jelly.

"Buenos días, you better be quick as Carlos your guide is already waiting outside."

There was a small bus waiting by the front, with a few more people that were going to join us in our hiking quest, and a few more stops latter on we picked up Richard and Clara.

"Good morning, guys, lovely to see you," said Richard as he boarded the bus.

"Ready for our adventure, my friend?" Erik asked.

They sat next to us; it felt as if we had known each other all our lives.

We arrived at the starting point and there were other people waiting, we were 14 people starting the Inca Trail; of all ages and from all over the world. We had to show our passports, before crossing the Urubamba River on a swaying bridge before we could begin our trek. The scenery had gone from awesome to astonishing, there were some very steep climbs, with some awkward descents.

The vegetation was lovely; aloe vera plants clinging to the mountains, prickly pears, trees with bunches of red pods, shrubs with bright yellow flowers, and lots of trees of white and yellow angel trumpet flowers growing everywhere in the wild made the place magical. The sound was also enchanting with the constant sound of a rushing river at a distance, and the sound of many birds and the occasional animal minding their own business, but the vistas were just to die for, with glimpses of snowy peaks along the Andean chain.

We saw people working in a partially restored Inca settlement right by a river that had stone terracing for agriculture; we also crossed a few villages with people all wearing colourful clothes and children playing and laughing and lots of alpaca herds.

After many hours walking, a few stops to rest and snack, we finally arrived at our campsite. The tents were already set up with the correct bags inside each one, we sat for dinner around a fire, and the porters had prepared a delicious meal and gave us all warm water for us to wash. Everyone was in high spirits.

It was a very clear night; with lots of bright shining stars some shooting across the dark sky, and the Milky Way was clearly visible.

I had kept a distance throughout the day, as I did when I walked the Camino de Santiago in Spain a few years ago. I was thinking about what Pedro had said and about Erik and what would happen after I left in a few days' time, but most of all I couldn't get Linda out of my mind, I thought Tom would never leave his wife and marry her, and bringing up a baby again by herself at her age; her husband had left her with her two sons when they were very young and now, this, poor Linda, I could feel the rejection as if it was happening to me, I felt guilty as I had left her in that job with Tom.

At that moment Erik came and hugged me. "Hello stranger, I've noticed you wanting to be by yourself so didn't want to intrude, but I hope you are not having second thoughts about me."

I gave him a big kiss. "I have been thinking of what is going to happen when I return back to London in only a few days', but mostly I've been thinking about my friend Linda." I told Erik all about her, and how much she relied on her income and how lonely she must be feeling right now.

"It's good to know that you weren't thinking about how to get rid of me, maybe pushing me down a cliff, please don't worry about our future, maybe Linda can help me out."

"How is Linda going to help us out?"

"Well, I've been thinking I will open an office in London and your friend Linda sounds like the perfect person to help me run it, she can say goodbye to Tom and his job and come and work for me, I will give her maternity leave, work from home, no need to worry, and you Dear Gaby, enjoy what is happening here, enjoy this magical place, we should be looking to see if we can catch a glimpse of our friends from the sky. Richard and Clara are really interesting and from Machu Picchu they are going to see the Nazca lines in the dessert in southern Peru, maybe we can go with them, you will only need to extend your stay for a few days, please say yes."

"Wow, that would be wonderful."

"So that means yes!"

"I mean wonderful that you can offer a job to Linda and thinking of having a base in London." I gave him a big hug, as if I never wanted to let go.

"And Nazca, I will have to think about it, there is George, the Yoga Centre, Linda, my flights, too many things to think about before I can say yes."

"At least it's good to know that you will consider it. That is another place that sounds like it was definitely built by our friends from the sky."

"As much as I would like to look out for spaceships, I am so tired that all I want is to get inside my sleeping bag," I said looking as if wouldn't even make it to our tent.

We started very early the following day, it was a gruelling walk towards the Dead Woman's Pass, the highest point of the Inca Trail at 4.200 metres, and I can see why it was called that. I was nearly dead when we reached the pass, and to see the porters having to carry all the tents, sleeping bags, food, water, cutlery and our luggage made me feel guilty, after eight hours of walking we finally reached the campsite, some of the porters that had walked ahead of us, greeted us with applause, helped us take our boots off and gave each of us a bowl of warm water to put our feet in. What a bunch of nice people, never complained and so happy to help us all. I barely made it to dinner and went straight to sleep.

Day three of the trek started with a very demanding uphill trek, my feet were really hurting and I was very short of breath, I could see that I wasn't the only one struggling, after a couple hours walking, Clara was starting to feel dizzy and Richard managed to hold her before she passed out. The head porter Luis gave her oxygen. After she recovered we had a long rest near a lagoon where there were some Inca ruins and Luis said it was a sacred sight. Luis had asked us to bring a stone or crystal to bury there, a bit like we did at the Cruz del Fierro in the Camino, he performed a short ceremony, we all held our hands and thanked the Apu of the place and one of the porters dug a small hole on the ground and we buried all our stones. Meanwhile one of them prepared some tea with special leaves including coca leaves, roots and some herbs and gave it to Clara, soon after she perked up and was ready climb Mount Everest.

With all the extra stops and the difficult climbs, we soon realized that we wouldn't get to camp in daylight. The weather was very foggy and the walking very slow, some of the porters that had walked ahead came back with torches to help us out. We passed through a dark tunnel, the stone path was full of twists and turns, up and down; I really had to pay attention where to place my feet. Eventually, as darkness fell, we made it to the campsite.

Finally, the last day of The Inca Trail, we climbed towards the Sun Gate and arrived there just as the sun was rising and it was quite a view. There, amongst the sun rays, we caught our first glimpse of Machu Picchu. What an achievement!

I held on to Erik and thought that if we had managed to get through those four days, we could get through anything in life.

It took another 45 minutes to walk down to the actual site, my poor thighs... Along the way, we met other people coming towards us who were clean, wearing smart clothes and shoes, who must have wondered who this scruffy lot were. They had arrived by train while were walking up to the Sun Gate.

I said to Erik: "If we ever come back here, I will do so by train!"

Luis guided us through the lost city, stopping in all the important places. It was all quite amazing and more so because it was built in such a remote and high area of the Andes, clearly it was meant as a very special place off the sight of the Conquistadors. It's a fascinating place, worthy of all its fame and recognition. On the way out we had our passports stamped with a Machu Picchu Seal, and worth all the effort of having walked the trail. We then boarded a bus to Aguas Calientes.

Most of us were staying at the same hotel but we had to say goodbye to Luis and all the wonderful porters, we all shed a few tears; it is amazing how a gruelling trek as the Inca Trail brings everyone closer and it makes you appreciate the good things in life. It's like when you talk to the old people that had been in World War II back in the UK; they all say they missed the sense of togetherness that those difficult years brought amongst the people and held the country together through such tough times. I turned round and said to Erik: "The magic of this world lies in its duality, the light cannot exist without the darkness, the stars would never shine so bright without the darkness of the sky, so always find the light that lies within the darkness and allow the light to shine through you, especially during difficult times."

"That is so beautiful, I undoubtedly feel much closer to you, my beacon of light."

The hotel staff had given us a quiet room at the back, and our suitcases were already there. Beds with sheets and duvets, proper bathroom, oh, how I had dreamt of having a shower. We were all clean and lying in our beds; aching, tired but very happy.

The next morning, we strolled around the quaint town of Aguas Calientes. Its name stems from the fact that there are thermal baths at the edge of the village, we all had a very relaxing deep bath in the soothing waters and had a massage afterwards, absolute heaven!

"So, what have you decided about Nazca, if you would like to go, we have to make reservations" asked Clara.

"I have to phone London and there are all the flights, etc. to sort out first, will go back to the hotel and let you know at dinner tonight."

"It would be great if you can come, and when will you get the chance to be back here in Peru?"

"We better get back and start the ball rolling," said a very enthusiastic Erik.

It always amazes me to think how small the world is now a days and how we are all connected at the touch of a button to all corners of the world, even from such a remote village as Aguas Caliente.

Back at the hotel I called George first:

"Hi, George..." and before I could even open my mouth, he said:

"If you want to stay longer, the answer is yes!"

"You know me well."

"I know you wouldn't call for anything else, and I know you are well and happy as Lucia spoke with Pedro, and he updated us on your trip, and Erik, he really likes him, especially as he gave him a very hefty tip. I will only worry if you are thinking of moving to Canada."

"World is so small now and good news travel fast, and don't worry. I'm staying put in London. Big hug to you and Lucia, I will let you know when I'm coming back as soon as I 've booked a return ticket."

Erik was already cancelling my ticket to London, even before I said anything.

"I won't book anything yet until we know exactly what we are doing next. I will call my office just to let them know they have a bit of a longer holiday before the boss returns."

Calling Linda was more difficult as I knew she needed me there with her, she answered the phone straight away:

"Hi darling when are you coming back, or have I lost my friend forever?"

"Hi gorgeous, how is baby and all with Tom, have you spoken with him?"

"Gaby, you probably know Tom will never leave his rich wife, he just wants me to have an abortion and go back to how things were, me doing all the work and he playing golf with a bit of sex now and then.

I'm worried about my income, how I'm going to support me, the boys and my baby?"

I had Linda on loud speaker so Erik could hear.

"Linda, this is Erik, you new boss, just give your notice in and as from today you are employed by me, how much do you currently earn?"

"£30.000 a year."

"Is that all? I will double your salary, I need to open an office in London and I would like you to manage it for me, I will give you maternity leave and from now you can work from home, I will send you all the information regarding my company and your role, I will ask my manager in Toronto to give you a call. Do you think you are fit to travel to Canada when I get back so we can work a plan as how to move forward?"

"Is this for real?"

"This is for real, Linda; you don't have to worry about your future," I said to her.

"I can't thank you enough, I can't wait to hand in my notice but I will do it in person because I want to see the bastard's face, when I tell him I'm leaving."

"That's my girl!"

"Erik, thank you, I will start looking into your company and see how we can make it work here in the UK. I won't let you down, if Jacinda Arden can manage a country with a new baby, I'm sure I can run your company and make it work."

"I don't doubt it."

"Big kisses Linda, I will call you again soon when I know for sure when I am coming back."

"Love you."

"I can't believe the bastard was paying her so little." Erik was livid.

"So, you are moving to London?"

"Not permanently but I told you we can work things out. Pedro has high hopes for us and so do I."

"We better go and talk to Clara and Richard so we can sort this trip to Nazca." I said getting straight up, as I was risking staying an extra day in Aguas Calientes if I didn't run downstairs.

We met up with them in the lobby of the hotel and went out to find a nice restaurant to have dinner and for them to tell us all about Nazca.

"We go back tomorrow by train to Cusco, we spend the night there and we fly to Arequipa in LATAM Airlines the following day at 8:30am, it's nearly a two hours flight, we spent one night in Arequipa and then take the bus to Nazca via the costal route, it's a 6-8 hours trip and then 2 days in Nazca, there we can book a flight to see the lines and back to Lima on a bus."

"There are no flights to Nazca?" asked Erik.

"I'm afraid there are no commercial flights as the airport there is only a very small one used solely for the small planes that fly over the lines."

"That's about an extra week here in Peru before I can return to London."

"About that, why don't you fly with us to Colombia, we can then fly back to London together, Richard wants to go to the Lost city in the Sierra Nevada, and speak with the Arhuaco Indians, they are an amazing tribe, that are guarding the Earth, you will love it and it will be just extra week, think about it." Clara was nearly pleading with us to join them.

"For now, I will book the flights to Arequipa and will leave the London one still open, tell me more about the Arhuaco tribe," I winked back at Clara.

"My sister was very ill a couple of years ago, she had been diagnosed with a degenerative condition and her prognosis was not good, after trying everything western medicine could offer, a friend of hers mentioned the Arhuaco, so as she had nothing to lose, she decided to go and see them. They live in the northern part of Colombia in the Sierra Nevada de Santa Marta Mountains. They consider those mountains to be the heart of the world, and believe that the well-being of the rest of the world depends on them. Their territory was vast, but they lost most of it during the Spanish colonization as the Incas did here in Peru and nowadays due to farming, marihuana and coca plantation and the government. They are a very peaceful tribe; they wear white tunics woven from sheep's wool that represent snow and cone-shaped hats emulating snowy peaks. They live mainly from agriculture and they sell woven mochilas that have become very trendy to wear by western Colombians. The tribe have Mamos that are selected by the elders when they are around eight or ten years old, receiving training for a minimum of nine years to around fifteen years. They live in a cave while the elders teach them everything they need to know about nature, herbs and healing. My sister spent many months living with them; she is now completely healed, and has learnt a lot from them and tries to spread their knowledge as much as she can.

The Arhuaco Mamos have been saying for years that the Earth would be plagued with "unknown illnesses" along with climate change and water and food shortages; as a consequence of the environmentally destructive practices of the "Younger Brothers" and that we must return to live by the Laws of Nature. In 1990, they opened their territory for the first time to outsiders, inviting a BBC film crew that made a documentary film called "From the Heart of the World: Elder Brothers' Warning." You should watch it when you get back to London.

"Wow they sound mesmerising, but I will love to spend a lot longer with them that a quick round trip, I think I will leave it for another time, when I can go and stay there for a long while, maybe going there with your sister, but I promise you I will watch that film as soon as I get back home."

"Richard, are you going?" asked Erik.

"Yes, I am, I would also like to spend more time there but I haven't got more paid holidays, but I want to go there anyway..."

"Then I might join you if I may, Colombia is on my way to Canada and I will also like to go and see them and the Arhuaco. Then I will be able to convince Gaby to go and stay with them another time."

"That will be great my friend, by all means join us, you are very welcome."

"Right, we better go to our room and book all the flights and bus journeys; I'll see you in the train back to Cusco." We all started walking back to the hotel and joking about all the things we were going to see in our trip.

Back in our room, Erik got the laptop out and started booking everything:

"Are you sure you don't want to go to Colombia?"

"I'm sure, I really want to get back to London and see Linda and George."

"OK, I will book your flight back home to London, but you can always change your mind if you want to."

The next day we took the train back to Cusco, the train had very large windows on each side to allow the passengers to admire the wonderful views. It went very slowly embracing the Andes, the cliffs below with never-ending abysses that made my stomach cringe, but it was a wonderful journey.

Nazca

Early the next day we took the flight to Arequipa, the city of the eternal blue sky. It was lovely to step out of the plane and feel the warm breeze caressing my face. I was holding Erik's hand and looked at him; I never thought I would ever feel so happy with a man, for the first time I wasn't longing for any more. I was just happy.

Arequipa is in southern Peru. It's the seat of the Constitutional Court of Peru and often dubbed the "legal capital of Peru". It is the second most populated city after Lima; it is famous for its incredible colonial legacy and its rugged natural landscape surrounded by volcanos.

We left our bags in the hotel and jumped in a hop on hop of bus and spent all day sightseeing the beautiful white colonial city. I was amazed at how imposing the city was; we ended our day roaming around the market and had the most fantastic carefree day.

The following day we took a bus to the Colca Canyon to admire the condors, the largest flying bird in their natural habitat. It was so amazing to watch them gliding through the air so close to us, and the views of the mountains and volcanoes were just breath-taking. On our way there we saw lots of llamas, alpacas and vicuñas. Another amazing day in beautiful Peru.

After that we took the bus from Arequipa to Nazca. It took around eight hours along the whole Pacific Coast of Peru; the bus was very comfortable, with air-conditioning, TV screens and WIFI; I took the opportunity to replay to all the messages I had been ignoring throughout my trip, I told Linda and George all about Erik and how happy I was, I wrote back to some of my other friends and clients, I was both happy and sad that I would soon be going back home to London. Erik was also writing lots, and lots of emails, he said he had written to everyone about me, and I could also feel how happy he was.

We arrived at Nazca very late at night and checked into our hotel. it had a lovely swimming pool, and as it was a very warm evening, we jumped in it; the sky was very clear and there were lots of starts, we saw a few shooting stars and some moving in the sky, everyone was excited as they all thought they were spaceships but I wasn't that convinced, they could have been satellites cruising around earth.

We woke up early and went to the reception to try and find an agency that could take us by plane to see the lines, and when we got to the lobby, we were immediately surrounded by lots of tour guide representatives trying to sell us their tour. Richard and Erik organized everything and soon we found ourselves in the back of a van heading towards the airport. The scenery was very arid as the Nazca Lines are located in the desert plains of the Rio Grande basin, an archaeological site that spans more than 75,000 hectares and is one of the driest places on Earth.

We arrived at the airport and the pilot came to greet us, there was another couple that was going to be on our flight; when I saw the small single engine aircraft, it gave me the creeps to think that I was going up in such a small plane. Erik, sensing that I was frightened, squeezed my hand.

"Don't worry; these guys have been doing this flight every day for many years."

"Five years; you are in safe hands with me," the pilot shouted as he overheard Erik.

We boarded the small plane; he asked us all to take a window each.

"I will fly-pass the lines from both sides so you can all take a good look at them."

We started taxing along the runway and up we went, I felt as if I was going up a roller-coaster, the plane was going up and down and the pilot started manoeuvring the plane, turning slightly to my side of the plane, and I thought I was going to fall off, then I looked at the lines and the pilot started telling us their story:

"The lines were created between 500 BC by people making incisions in the desert floor, removing pebbles and leaving differently coloured dirt exposed. Some trenches go on for as much as 30 miles, slicing great parallel lines across the desert. The Nazca Lines represent about 70 animals and plants, some of which measure up to 370 meters long, there is a spider, hummingbird, cactus plant, monkey, whale, llama, duck, flower, tree, lizard and a dog, there is a humanoid figure nicknamed "The Astronaut", hence all the stories about them being built by extra-terrestrials.

The first travellers who stumbled upon them in the 1500s thought they were the remnants of roads from a long-gone civilization. It wasn't until 1927 that the truth was discovered. Peruvian archaeologist Toribio Mejía was making his way up a series of nearby hills when he glanced down and saw the undulations in the valley below; he realized they weren't the ruins of ancient roads at all. They were a set of massive images, symbols carved into the earth, so big that they were unrecognizable from ground level.

So, it began almost a century of investigation as archaeologists and amateur enthusiasts alike tried to make sense of one of the world's greatest mysteries. The Nazca Lines have inspired countless theories about their origin. Are they extra-terrestrial, a message from ancient civilizations, do the geoglyphs have an astronomy-related purpose? No one really knows."

"What do you think they are, as you have spent so many years flying over them?" asked one of the other passengers.

"If I knew I wouldn't be here, I would be rich and famous having exposed one of the greatest enigmas on Earth, but I don't know how they could have been done, in an era before Christ, if they couldn't fly. When we land, I suggest you go on one of the tours that show you the lines from the ground and you will realize that it's impossible to make up these magnificent geoglyphs if you can't fly, it does really make you wander if they were built by extra-terrestrials."

We all took another look and just wandered the same thing.

When we landed, we did just that, we took a tour around the lines from the ground, we walked around them and we reached the same conclusion, they must have had help from our friends from the sky.

That evening when we were having dinner, everyone was very excited and all wanted to take another flight to see the lines from above one more time, before heading back to Lima.

The following morning, we headed straight to the airport and our pilot greeted us with a big smile.

"Buenos días amigos, I gather you want to take a second look round the lines? I never get bored of them and I always discover new things whenever I look at them."

We boarded the small aircraft, this time it was just the four of us, I was even more nervous that the previous day; just the thought of going back up in that roller-coaster flight made my stomach cringe. This time the pilot went up a bit higher in the sky, he wanted to show us the vastness of the whole area and how it made even more sense the higher we went. The plane started tossing and shaking and then the engine totally died. I also started shaking and Erik jumped into the seat next to mine, he put his arms around me and tried to calm me down.

"Don't worry, these planes can glide for a long time and will manage to land with no problem." He whispered in my ear: "I love you".

I heard the pilot calling the tower "mayday, mayday" we were losing altitude pretty fast and I could feel that we wouldn't make it; the plane started to shake violently. I closed my eyes and then I heard a big bang. Erik was holding me really tight; I remember being thrown out of the plane after impact, but I don't recall anything after that.

A while later I heard a voice shouting: "this one is alive, this one is alive." There was a big commotion around me and could feel that I was being put into a stretcher and I was then whisked up in a helicopter, I kept fading in and out of consciousness while a voice was gently asking me to stay awake. I was flown into a nearby military hospital and rushed into the operating theatre; there I popped out of my body and was watching all the doctors desperately working around my body that was lying lifeless on the operating table. I then watched the screen when I flatlined.

I was there watching my body but I couldn't relate to it anymore, I then went through a portal that was so seductive that I was pushed right inside it and travelled through a long tunnel following the light to the other side. I saw lots of planets and galaxies; I could see the whole universe and stars so bright that I was almost blinded by them, it was the most beautiful thing I had ever seen, I could also hear the most magnificent music that as I had never heard before; I then I had the feeling that I wasn't alone, I sensed a presence that surrounded me and embraced me and then he said:

"I've known you; I have always loved you, as I love every single person in the universe".

He then showed me how we are all connected. There is a light that emanates from him, that is within each one of us and we are all made from the same beautiful beam of light. I was astonished by it all and all I could feel was this amazing unconditional love like no other.

I then saw my whole life, I was shown everything that I had done, I felt the pain that I had caused to others due to my actions, but I felt it from their own point of view, as if I was them, and a sense of guilt and remorse invaded me, and thought that I had made huge mistakes in my life, the presence, our God our Creator that was standing right there next to me said:

"There are no mistakes, only lessons, what did you learn from it?"

He was not judging me, only love emanated from him, I was also shown the good that I had done and how that vibration had touched everyone around me, I realized the importance of how even the most insignificant things have such a an outstanding positive effect, like when I helped an old lady cross the street, or gave my seat to a pregnant woman when she boarded a train, those things create such a ripple of goodness that I wished I had made a point of helping more. But I was now in this place where there was only love, bliss, and beauty that went right through me, making me feel joyful and felt that I was finally home, really home and all the longing had vanished.

I then saw Erik, I rushed to him and we embraced. I knew then that we had been together many lifetimes in many galaxies, and that we were united for infinity, I was whole. He looked at me and said:

"You have to go back."

"But why?" I was so surprised by his request, I did not want to leave him nor did I want to leave heaven, I didn't want to go back.

He put his hands on my belly "You are carrying our child, our daughter" I looked down and I could see this tiny sparkle, blinking within me.

"She is part of the army of angelic children being born now to help earth through this tough transition, she will shine her light in all the corners of the earth."

"Then come back with me?" I pleaded with him.

"I can't go back now, but I will be with you always, you will feel and hear me, everywhere, I will be waiting for you and we will be together for eternity as we have always been and always will be."

I looked at God asking him what to do. "You must return, you have a purpose in this life that you have not yet fulfilled, you chose this event to happen in your life, as from this point onwards you will start to follow your real path, go and spread my love". I understood then that I had to go back; I kissed Erik and in a blink of an eye I was back in the operating theatre, I was standing next to an angel that I believe was to be my daughter, we were watching together as the doctors were working on my body, I could see that there were other angels behind every doctor and nurse in that room, sending healing energy through them to my body, and then the flatline on the screen started jumping again and I went back into my body.

I'm not sure how many days I spent in a coma, but when I came round, I saw Pedro seating right next to me and holding my hand.

"Welcome back," he said in a very soft voice.

My body ached all over and it was very difficult to even open my mouth.

"What are you doing here?"

"Lucia phoned me; the consulate contacted George as you gave him as your next of kin in your travel documents."

"Pedro, you said the Apus have said we were going to be together always, and he is gone, he is already home," I said to him with tears in my eyes.

"How do you know; you've been in a coma for a week?"

"I saw him on the other side, I didn't want to leave him, but he urged me to do so, I'm having his baby daughter," I wasn't sure if I should have said anything.

"You will always be together, not it the way that you have thought you would be, but closer than you can ever imagine."

And then I heard Erik's voice loud and clear in my head.

"I am here right next to you," and I could feel him smiling.

Pedro squeezed my hand as if he had heard him too, and then the nurses came in and all started rushing around me and called the doctor. They asked Pedro to leave the room, and I asked them not to send him away, as I wanted him close to me. I could feel his energy and how soothing it was to have him nearby. I felt different than before my Near-Death-

Experience, as if something inside me had changed. In fact, everything had changed, I viewed the world from a different perspective, I wasn't afraid of dying I now knew that the other side was more real than this one, and that I was a soul having an experience here on earth, just to learn and be closer to God, that we all came from him and we were all bound together by his energy.

I tried to tell the doctor and the nurses about my experience and that I would be fine as God had said I had told me I had purpose to fulfil, and they all looked at me as if I was absolutely nuts. Pedro asked me not to say anything but I was elated and wanted to shout to the world all I had seen and learnt but, after a few days I knew that Pedro was right and that it was best not to say anything.

I was told that the only other survivor was the pilot but he was in another hospital but Clara and Richard had also perished in the accident.

The first person to call was George.

"I am so happy to hear your voice, I've been so worried, I am trying to sort out things here and flights so I can come and be there with you."

"Please don't come, there is nothing you can do here, I am very well looked after and Pedro has been like an angel sent by God to look after me, I am sure of that. Soon I will be flown to a hospital in Lima and when I am able to do the long hall flight, I will be home in London. The consulate has been in touch too and they are making sure that I get all the treatment I need." I tried to sound very reassuring. "Please call

Linda and make sure she is alright, I don't want to talk to anyone right now, it's all very painful, as you can imagine, is not just the body that needs to heal but the soul too."

"I understand, I will ask Pedro to keep me informed on a daily basis." I handed over the mobile to Pedro.

"Pedro, I don't know how I am going to repay you, for all your time and dedication."

"Don't worry Gaby, Erik gave me such a big tip, that I am sure his soul already knew what was coming and that you would need me here with you, so I am not going anywhere and you don't owe me anything."

"What happened to Erik's body?" It was the first time I had actually asked about him; sometimes I thought that my NDE was just a dream.

"His mother flew here on a private jet soon after the accident and took him back to Canada."

"She took my body but I am right here with you," I heard Erik's voice again.

"I think I am losing my mind Pedro; I keep hearing his voice."

"You are not losing your mind, I can hear him too, as I can hear other spirits and the Apus, and soon you will learn how to "listen" to him and others as I do."

Pedro kept a vigil day and night, he brought me herbal medicines and performed chanting and filled my body with energy. I was flown with him in an army airplane to Lima, where the Consul was waiting for me and took me to a nearby hospital until I was well enough to fly back home to London.

Saying goodbye to Pedro was very hard.

"We will meet again, Gaby, and will be in touch always, I will be sending you distant healing, you have to find a balance between the doctor's medicine and alternative healing, look for people that can help you in the Isles of Avalon, you will need it; it's very important to work hand in hand with both medicines, the doctors will fix your bones and your body but a Shaman, a healer like me must help you heal your aura and your soul." He gave me a big hug and kissed me on my forehead.

I was flying first class and the flight attendants were especially careful with me, I still had a cast on one arm and one leg, a few bandages on my head and a corset all around my chest as I had broken a few ribs. The captain came by to greet me.

"I will try and stay away from turbulence; the weather forecast is good so we should have a smooth ride all the way to London."

"Captain, can you do me a favour; can you please sign my cast?"

He smiled at me, took out his pen and signed it. I could see everyone staring at me, I knew the accident had been all over the news and some of the passengers came to say hello and also signed the cast during the flight. I had been given strong painkillers by the hospital and some sleeping pills, and before I knew it, the plane was landing in London.

London

An ambulance was waiting for me right next to the airplane. I was the last passenger to leave the plane and was lowered down via the food loading platform straight to a stretcher and into the ambulance that took me to St Thomas' Hospital, right in front of the river Thames and the Houses of Parliament.

I was taken to the A&E at the hospital and was greeted by a doctor who was waiting for my arrival.

"How are you feeling?"

"I think I am pregnant," I said. It was the first time I had mentioned the possibility of my pregnancy.

The nurses quickly took a urine sample and soon enough she said: "It's positive." They all looked at me, thinking how could it be possible that on top of all my injuries, they now had to care for a pregnant woman.

"Who is the father?" asked the doctor looking very concerned.

"He perished during the accident." I said now with tears on my eyes.

"Do you want to keep it? It is only going to put more strain on to your body during your recovery."

"She is the only reason I'm alive."

"So, it's going to be a girl?"

"I'm sure it's going to be a baby girl," I said now smiling and looking rather proud.

"We are going to remove all this heavy plaster casts and put you into lighter and softer coverings; especially the corset, now that you have that extra passenger; and a foot fracture walking boot will allow you to start moving and commence rehabilitation."

"Please, remove the cast on my arm carefully; I would like to keep it as a memento of what happened to me."

I felt so much better, and now that I was covered in plastic and not plaster and with the help of the nurses, I managed to have a shower, I had never felt so good since the accident. I had new bandages put around my head; I was still bruised all over but not as swollen. I was taken to my ward and was sharing a room with 4 other ladies. My bed was next to the window, overlooking the Thames and the beautiful Houses of Parliament, I felt happy to be alive but was overcome with sadness thinking of everything that had happened to me, and as I was closing my eyes, I heard a scream.

"Darling Gaby!" Linda was running towards me, "Finally I was allowed in to see you, I have been waiting all morning." She gave me a big hug and started sobbing.

"Don't cry, I am still here, let me see your bump, you are looking as beautiful and glamorous as usual." But Linda wouldn't stop hugging me; I stroked her hair until she calmed down.

"I am so sorry I made you lose your job."

"I should have done it years ago." Linda immediately perked up. "At least I kept the 4x4 and Tom gave me a substantial, let's say "bribe" package so I don't tell his wife."

"The bastard!"

"But nature has a great revenge prepared for him, you know he has three girls and always wanted a boy, and now I am expecting one." Now Linda was looking as wicked as always.

"And I have a surprise for you… I am expecting a girl."

"Noooooo way!" she screamed so loud that everyone turned to look at us.

"When did you find out?"

"Just now."

"But it's too early to know if it's a girl?"

"I just know and I am going to call her Erika."

"Oh, Darling, and we can't even drink Prosecco to celebrate, couple of Old Age Pensioners pregnant", we burst out laughing. I think it was the first time I had laughed since the accident, better medicine in life and that's why I loved Linda so much.

I spent a couple of weeks in hospital, all my friends and George kept visiting me, keeping me company and trying to do their best to perk me up. Lucia came in one day looking rather happy.

"I am also pregnant Gaby; it looks as we are going to need a nursery at the yoga centre."

"Wow, that is very good news, I am really happy, I bet Luna can't wait to meet her brother or sister."

"And, that is not all the good news; Margarita is coming to London next week, she is traveling with Scott, they will be stopping here on their way to Scotland to meet his family; it looks like we will be attending a wedding soon; she sends you lots of love."

"Wow, that it's also great news, I will love to see them, I think I will be allowed to go home soon, I am working very hard on the physio and Pedro has been sending lots of distant healing."

"Who is going to help you at home? You can't stay there on your own," said Lucia looking a bit concerned.

"I have asked George to make some inquiries around the centre, I don't want just anyone to come and clean the house, I would like someone to help me lift my soul."

"You have lots to look forward to," Lucia said touching my belly.

"We all have something to look forward to darlings," said Linda as she walked in a joined us.

"You knew Lucia was pregnant and you didn't tell me anything."

"It was so hard to keep the secret darling, but we all thought it best if Lucia told you herself. But!"

"But… This sounds serious. I know that tone of voice," I said now looking pretty worried.

"When are you going to tell Erik's Mum?"

"Yes, when are you going to tell my Mum? That would also give her something to look forward to," I heard Erik's voice in my head once again, and I started looking around.

"Have you lost something?" asked Lucia.

"No, sorry."

"Don't get distracted darling; when are you going to tell Erik's Mum? I still have the emails his company sent me when he offered me the job; I can write to them and say you would like to get in touch with her." Linda said whilst pulling my laptop out of her handbag.

I held my laptop as if I was back in touch with an old friend. "I'll have to think about it, I can't even remember her name."

"Elizabeth, Lizzy" I heard him say.

I started crying, "It's going to be hard."

"Take your time, but I think you must."

"Visiting time is nearly over," came the announcement over the loudspeaker.

I hugged them both and I stayed looking at my laptop, so far, I had not looked at my emails, or social media; I opened my Facebook account and there were hundreds of messages all wishing me well from people I didn't even know. I was overwhelmed by the outpouring of love from all of them; there was one in particular that caught my eye.

"Hello Gaby, I am Clara's sister Lilly. I am in London as I came here for Richard's funeral, and would love to see you, please send me a private message via messenger."

"Hi Lilly, I am at St Thomas's hospital, please come as I would love to see you too."

The nurse came in, "Time to go to sleep, I am afraid you have to put your laptop away now." I turned it off, and fell as sleep soon after.

At 2 pm the following day as the visitors' time started, a woman walked in through the door that was the spitting image of Clara, she came running towards me and gave me a big hug.

"So wonderful to finally meet you Gaby, Clara mentioned you in all her final messages."

"Lovely to meet you too Lilly, Clara talked a lot about you and the Arhuaco Indians and she and Richard were really looking forward to seeing you."

"Richard's funeral was yesterday but I kept some of his ashes as I would like to throw them together with some of Clara's in the Sierra Nevada in Colombia."

"I think they would like that, maybe I can go with you when I get better."

"When are you leaving this hospital?"

"I am sure the doctors would let me go now, but I need to find a carer."

"I can look after you," she said it out loud and I knew it was coming from her heart.

"I can help you recover too, with herbs and healing I learnt from the Arhuaco."

"Are you sure, it won't be too much for you?"

"I would love to".

"So that is settled. Nurse! I am going home."

The following day George came to pick me up at the hospital. I said farewell to all the lovely nurses that had helped looking after me there; nurses are really an army of angels sent by God to this earth, they have a soul like no one else, they do help people recover not just physically but mentally too, they have very special purpose and often difficult path that goes unrecognized most of the time.

We drove through London, I just stared at this marvellous city with so much history and so resilient; the traffic was quite heavy but we finally made it home, and as I opened the front door to my flat, Linda, Lucia and Lilly were inside, they had flowers and incense burning and it felt wonderful to finally be home. Lilly had set herself in the spare room, she felt as if she was already part of the family and perfect for me at this time in my life, another angel sent straight from heaven. The next few days Lilly helped a lot using herbs and gave me healing with her hands; it was a sort of Reiki healing. She also used bells and drums.

"The Arhuaco Shaman said that the sound vibrations are very important in order to align our bodies and keep the energy flowing around us, which is why most Indian civilizations use drums in all their ceremonies."

"There is a lady at the centre that does sound healing with bowls and gongs, maybe I will ask her to come here one day."

"That would be fantastic."

She also game me herbal medicine to help me boost my energy, I told her I had not taken any medicines at the hospital because I didn't want to harm my baby.

"Don't worry I will only give you natural herbs."

"The word "natural" doesn't mean that they are safe, there are many plants out there that are harmful. Here in the UK mushrooms have become very popular; not only for recreational purposes but for healing too but, mushrooms can also kill you."

"I learnt from a very good Shaman and I wouldn't give you anything to harm you or the baby, I spent two years up in the mountains and I really want to help people use less conventional medicines and look up to nature. The pharmaceutical industries don't want to cure you; they make their money by getting you addicted to medicines, claiming to cure you, and when the side effects of medicines kick in, they give you something else to counteract and soon you will end up taking bags of pills that are depleting your body of all its own power to heal itself and leave you even without the will to live. That happened to me, I was blown up like a balloon, with steroids and medicines that were killing me; I was fat and ugly and I had no more desire to keep walking on this earth, one day I had such a bad allergic reaction to one of the medicines the doctors had prescribed that I ended up in A&E. A friend came to my rescue, and took me to see the Arhuaco and I have never looked back. I threw away all the pills and took what nature has to offer and it's all for free."

"You look amazing, I can't imagine you fat and ugly and your skin and hair are like that of a young girl."

"Healthy eating is the answer to everything, bacteria live happily ever after in an unhealthy body, if you are strong there are less possibilities for you to catch an infection, and we stay looking younger longer. Water is also very important to the Arhuaco, they have been fighting with the Colombian authorities to try to keep their rivers clean and safe from pollution as the oil and gas companies around The Sierra Nevada dump very harmful waste on them. The Arhuaco say that water is a living entity and that we should ask it to heal us before we drink it." Lilly said that with a big smile, she was glowing and radiant. Whatever she ate I sure wanted it for me too.

I was improving lots each day, we started taking short strolls in the park and just sat by the tree in my garden meditating, I needed to heal my body, mind and spirit. I missed Erik.

"Reach out to Mum," I heard Erik's voice again. I called Linda and asked her for the emails.

"I have already written to Erik's manager, they are waiting for you to reach out to them, and don't give me "the look". She deserved to know that there is a grandchild on the way."

"You haven't said anything, have you?"

"Of course not, darling, that is for you to say, and the manager's name is also Tom, it seems as if I was swapping one Tom for another."

"Have you heard from him?"

"Only when he needs to find out something about work, but he never asks me how I am or the baby."

"Block him off Linda; let him struggle with his job!" I was furious.

"Calm down, that's why I don't mention him, Om-mmm."

"Forward me Canada's Tom's email and I promise I will write to him."

I kept staring at his email, but didn't know what to write. Lilly sat next to me and she wrote it for me.

"Dear Tom, I am Gaby, Erik's girlfriend, I am trying to reach out to his Mum, but I don't have her details and I would like you to help me contact her, this is my email and my phone number is +44 7939 2565 44."

"Now, you press the send button," Lilly said to me and I did. A few minutes later I received a call from a number I didn't recognize.

"Hello Gaby, I'm Lizzy, Erik's Mum." I started to cry and couldn't say a word, so she continued talking: "Erik talked nonstop about you since he met you; he was so happy, and I keep right next to me in bedside table the photo you took of him sitting next to an Indian woman in a bus in Bolivia, the happiest day of his life he said, he had just met you."

"Happiest day of my life too," I finally managed to say.

"Please send me all the photos you took of him and especially all the ones of you two together."

"Just tell her!" I heard his voice once again.

"Lizzy, I am pregnant; you are going to be a grandmother." I said it as gently as I could, but there was only silence on the other side of the line.

"Give her time," he whispered on my ear.

"Are you sure it's his?" she finally said.

"A hundred per cent."

"I must come and meet you both then."

"There are still seven months to go until I give birth." I said: "I'm trying to get better so I can cope with the birth although the doctors said it must be delivered by a Caesarean section as they think my body will be too fragile for a normal birth."

"Not if I can help it," I heard Lilly's voice in the background.

I hung up and sent her all the photos, I also put her in contact with Linda, so they could make all the arrangements for her to come over, she needed a place to stay and Linda and Canadian Tom though it was best if she stayed in a flat close to mine.

I was already walking by myself and looking much better by the time she was due to fly in, my belly was slightly visible and it had now been confirmed by the doctors that it would be a girl. I drove to Heathrow with Linda to pick her up at the airport, we must have looked a right sight as Linda was now enormous as she was due anytime soon, but she insisted on going to pick up Lizzy and C Tom up as they were flying in together. As soon as they came through the door, I could see Linda's face lit up.

"For goodness' sake Linda, you are nine months pregnant!"

"And my waters just broke." We hardly had time to greet each other and with C Tom now firmly on the driver's seat we went straight to St Thomas' Hospital. I was trying to calm Linda down on our way to the hospital and Lizzy couldn't stop looking at me, it wasn't exactly the way I had planned to greet her, but God always work in mysterious ways. We arrived at the hospital and we went straight to A&E; the nurses asked C Tom if he was the father; he didn't say anything and just walked straight in with her to the delivery room.

"Your friend really knows how to make a big impression on her first date out with a man," Lizzy said looking at me.

"It looks as if you will end up opening that office branch here in London quite soon," I said with a look of dismay staring at Linda and C Tom.

"Are you going in with her?"

"No, I can't face going in there, not yet."

We stayed talking just the two of us in the waiting room. It was just perfect, I told her all about our trip to Cusco and Machu Pichu, and I showed her my star.

"I wondered why he was wearing this", and she showed me his star. "We must give it to Erika, to wear so she can remember her Dad." It just hit me that she would never see her dad, and I just cried and cried. Lizzy kept stroking my hair until suddenly C Tom came into the waiting room holding baby Oliver in his arms.

"Linda wants you to take a picture and send it to her sons."

"They are already on their way here," I said. I held Oliver in my arms, he was so perfect.

"Soon you will be holding Erika in your arms, she is here with me, and she will always feel me around her, as I am here with you right now my love," Erik whispered again into my ear, I was getting used to hearing his voice right next to me.

When Linda's sons arrived, C Tom and Lizzy and I drove to their flat, it was just around the corner from mine, so I left them there and I walked back home.

Lilly was waiting for me, with a warm bowl of soup already on the table, I knew she would have to go back soon and I was dreading it, I had grown very fond of her and I don't think I could have recovered so swiftly if it had not been for her.

"You look very tired Gaby."

"I am," I told her all about Oliver's birth.

"Trust Linda to time things so well, what was she thinking driving all the way to Heathrow today when she was practically overdue."

"That is my Linda, and now that she can drink, she will probably be popping a bottle of Prosecco right now." We both laughed.

"Now that Lizzy is here, I will be booking my return flight, I must get back home and set Clara and Richard free."

I then heard their voices in my head: "Tell her we love her and that we are already free."

"You are always welcome here Lilly, you are part of the family now."

"I know but you also need to get the bedroom ready for Erika."

I gave her a big hug as if I didn't want to let her go, but then I knew it wouldn't be the last time I would see her.

Baby Erika

The first day that Lizzy went to my flat she just looked and looked around, I thought she was investigating to see if I had any hidden secrets.

"This is a very nice flat but is way too small for you and a baby," she finally said.

"It's big enough for both of us, I was perfectly fine living here with Lilly and it will be just great for me and Erika, I've lived here all my adult life and I love it here."

"I am just saying, it will be okay for now I guess," Lizzy said with a hint of irony in her voice; "We better go and buy all the things to fill it up."

We walked out towards my cherished blue and white convertible Mini, and Lizzy just stood there staring at it.

"How on earth are you going to fit a pram in here?" with a face of utter disbelief.

"This is my most precious possession, I'll make it work, there must be a fold up pram that can fit at the back," I said looking proudly at my beautiful Mini.

We went to Selfridges, a huge superstore in Oxford Street; at least I was sure Lizzy wouldn't find it too small. As we walked in the store, Lizzy saw some artwork on display on the shop windows.

"Is this an art gallery?"

"Selfridges promotes new and upcoming artists by showing their work on some of their windows."

"This is fantastic, what a great idea to help young talented artists giving them such a prominent position to display their artwork, all stores should do the same," I felt quite relieved thinking that at least she had approved that one.

Selfridges is a huge store; but we went straight to the maternity department. Lizzy was in her element choosing the cot, baby changing station, clothes, bottles, bath, towels, creams, nappies; you name it and she was just pointing at it, and it looked as she was ready to fit the whole store into my tiny flat.

"Lizzy, I can't afford all that, we have to prioritize what I really need, and what fits into the flat and my budget," I said trying to stop her going mad around the shop.

"Gaby, this is for my granddaughter."

"But she is my daughter too and I want do my best for her with what I have," I said pleading with her.

"I'm sorry Gaby, but at least let me help you."

In the end we reached a compromise and we paid half each. I could feel Erik giving a sigh of relief from the other side.

The nursery looked lovely and the day of the birth finally arrived, there was no drama, no rush, the date had been set by my friend from India, Dev Patel, as he had consulted with the top astrologers in Yogananda's Ashram, regarding the best time and date for Erika to be born at the perfect time, so that the stars aligned in her favour to set path towards having a beautiful life. The doctors had agreed after some persuasion to carry out the Caesarean section at the chosen time. George came to pick me and Lizzy at my home, and drove us to St Thomas Hospital, I kept touching my belly and couldn't wait to finally hold baby Erika in my arms. Lizzy was holding my arms, supporting me all the time, I don't know what I would have done without her, I had decided on an epidural so I could stay awake throughout the whole birth procedure. I could also feel Erik right next to me and finally Erika cried and took her first breath, I cried too of pure joy and thought that coming back to give birth to my baby girl was the best decision I had ever made and although Erik was not there with me in person, he would always be there for both of us guiding us and supporting us. Lizzy was also crying and when she held her, she said:

"She looks just like Erik when he was born."

"I still want a DNA test carried out, Lizzy, the nurse is going to take a swab from your mouth," I said looking at both of them.

"I have never doubted you, Gaby."

"It is not for you for, it is for the authorities, so she can bear Erik's surname in her birth certificate and have him registered as her father."

"I will gladly do that." She immediately opened her mouth and the nurse took a swab from her and baby Erika. The nurse explained that the results would take a couple of weeks and the lab would post them in a letter to my home address.

Lizzy went back to Toronto as she thought it was best to give me and Erika time to bond, and also because she had business to attend to. She had decided to open a branch of her company here in London and C Tom would manage it together with Linda and she needed to appoint a new manager for their office in Toronto.

Life with a new baby and on my own wasn't easy, I couldn't ask Linda for help as she was struggling with baby Oliver, but at least her sons and C Tom gave her a hand. Lucia came round from time to time but she was now heavily pregnant and was struggling too. As Lizzy had foreseen my small flat was proving to be too small for both of us; the whole place looked like a battle ground full of toys, nappies, bottles all over the floor, and on top of that I was very sleep-deprived and had no strength to clean it up and the whole place was a mess. I finally asked Lizzy if she could come and give me a hand. The letter from the DNA lab had arrived but I wanted her to be there with me so we could open it together.

Lizzy immediately agreed to come back to London; she didn't need much persuading as she was dying to see Erika. When she was due to arrive I couldn't go to Heathrow to pick her up as there was no room to fit a baby seat, pram, Lizzy and her luggage in my Mini, so it seemed that my precious car would have to go.

I was so happy to see her, and so was Erika, I just handed her to Lizzy and went for a much-needed sleep. When I woke up, Lizzy had managed to clean the flat, tidy, all up, and Erika was just all similes and no crying for Nana Lizzy.

"I bet you don't believe me now when I say that she cries all the time?"

"It's the energy; babies can feel the stress of their parents, especially a first-time mother like you who has been coping alone. Now let's open this envelope." Lizzy handed me the DNA lab envelope; I opened it very carefully and gave it straight back to her.

"I can't look; please you read what it says."

"The alleged grandmother is not excluded as the biological grandmother of the tested child based on testing results obtained from analysis of the DNA loci listed, the probability of Mrs Elizabeth Jenks being the grandparent is 99.9998%."

"Welcome Erika Jenks, let's go and register you right now, I would love to see Erik's name as her father on her birth certificate," I said looking very proudly at my baby daughter.

I came out of the register office looking at the document; I was so happy.

"You know what that means?" asked Lizzy.

"That Erik is her father, not just in my heart but under the law."

"That means that she is the sole heir of her father's estate and a very large estate it is."

"I didn't do it because of that." I was quite taken a back.

"But other people might think so, his ex-wife was trying to claim it and some other distant relatives also wanted to be included as he died without writing a will, but this puts an end to it."

"Tell her about your NDE", I heard Erik's voice on my head.

"Lizzy, I want to tell you about something that happened to me after the accident; you better sit down and listen with an open mind." I told her all about me popping out of my body whilst I flatlined during surgery, of meeting Erik and how he told me that I had to come back because I was pregnant, and that I knew it was going to be a girl even before it was confirmed by the doctors. I also told her that since then I could hear his voice and that of other spirits on the other side."

Lizzy stayed there not saying anything, not knowing what to make of all this. I said to Erik in my mind; "I shouldn't have said anything, she is now thinking I am crazy."

"Tell her about when she made me wear a blue velvet jacket for my prom and that she didn't allow me to take cooking classes at school as she thought it was too girlish and she made me take carpentry instead." I repeated the information to her.

"So, you can really hear him and life does go on."

"We are spirits having an earthly experience, in order to grow and dying is actually just returning home, the love I experienced there is like no other, and I know that being on that other realm is the easy part of our existence, what is very difficult is walking our path on this earth, I also know there are many other planets and we don't only incarnate here, but the earth is one of the planets where the learning is more difficult and challenging, and that we are about to embark on a massive spiritual awakening and the children being born now are part of an army of angels being sent here to help this transition. I know Erika has a difficult task ahead of her, and we must always be here to support her."

"Erik, tell Gaby that she has to move out of this flat, move to the countryside nearer to nature." Lizzy shouted looking upwards as if talking directly to Erik.

"She is right, Gaby; it's time to move on."

"He says you are right."

"Thank God for that, from now on I will always ask Erik for his advice."

I started searching in the internet for areas that wouldn't be too far from London or the M25 for easy access to Heathrow airport, for Lizzy's travelling to Toronto. I liked the idea of Herefordshire just north of the M25 between St. Albans and Garden City, far but not in the middle of nowhere. We looked at several properties around there and then I came across a converted barn, with a Granny annex. As soon as I reached the front door, I knew it would be the one. The door knocker was in the shape of a Vesica Pisces; just like the cover of the Chalice Wells in Glastonbury.

Moving was not an easy task, they say that the death of a dear person, having a baby and moving houses, are the most stressful things that can happen to you in this life, and all three had happened to me within a year, but it was all worth it, the space and the light of the barn were fantastic; having Lizzy living so close was great, and the gardens were just magnificent and so peaceful and relaxing, a far cry from my noisy flat in London, where you could hear the cracking of the floorboards from neighbours upstairs, the sirens of the police from time to time. I soon forgot about my little flat in north London. George had offered me money for my half of the yoga centre as he knew it would be difficult for me to go back to work and I didn't want to either, I wanted to spend as much time as possible with Erika.

I was in the garden one afternoon sitting in the lawn with Linda drinking a glass of our favourite Prosecco, it was just perfect.

"Who would have thought our lives would change so much, I used to chase every man and dream that passed in front of me and now, I just want to be here, no more running, and I am happy," I said to Linda while watching our toddlers play together.

"Darling, we should go and see the fortune-teller in Glastonbury again soon, maybe he can tell us what's going to happen to us next?"

"Have you heard about that virus that is going around in China? Apparently, they have locked everyone at home in a town called Wuhan," I said to Linda with a somewhat worried tone in my voice.

"Darling, China is on the other side of the world, why worry?"…

And then, the pandemic hit, all over the world, killing thousands of people and every country in the world had to go into lockdown, forcing us to look inwards and the massive awakening started.

Doris Plummer, born in Cali, Colombia, educated at the British School Colegio Colombo Británico, studied graphic design at the Jorge Tadeo Lozano University in Bogotá and moved to London where she worked at the Colombian Embassy. She later attained a Diploma in Public Service Interpreting at Westminster College in London and currently works for the British Courts and as a Conference Interpreter travelling extensively around the world. She has two sons, two wonderful daughters-in-law a beautiful granddaughter and grandson.

Email: dorisplummer5@gmail.com